THE MAN ON WORLD X

PROBLEM ONE: An Earthman is suddenly and mysteriously transposed to an alien planet: an utterly empty, completely lifeless outpost of a far-flung galaxy. The Earthman has no idea where he is, how he came to be on the godforsaken world, or how to get home.

PROBLEM TWO: For company there is only a computer: a computer which has all the answers to all of the Earthman's questions. But the computer is programmed to give information only to those properly trained and qualified to understand it. The Earthman is not.

SOLUTION: The Earthman must outwit the rigid electro-mechanical being to learn the secrets that will get him back to Earth . . . but the solution is the biggest problem of them all.

Shock
Wave

Walt & Leigh Richmond

WILDSIDE PRESS

To

The Scott
. . . the choice and the responsibility.

I

TERRY FERMAN rolled and twisted in the confines of his sleeping bag, then restrained himself from sitting up, realizing just in time that the camper was too small for such a hasty action.

Turning, he glanced out the small porthole. The huge trees beyond the tiny riverside clearing he'd chosen for his campsite were outlined, smoky gray against a dawn sky. As rapidly as possible in such a cramped space he struggled into the warm clothing necessary to this climate and made his way into the open to survey the tumbling waters of the Feather River and the green olivene cliffs beyond.

It would be a good day for fishing, he decided, and he had been allowing his studies at Berkeley to keep him far too long away from the mountain streams that were his first love; a priority that electronics should not be allowed to assume. But first there was the project for which he had come on this field trip.

He glanced again at the tall green cliffs. It would be quite a trick to get a signal out of this valley with his tiny transistorized transmitter, though he ought to be able to manage it with a long enough transmitting wire.

The project, for all that Cal had tried to make it mysterious, was simple enough—to pinpoint by radio direction the source of anomalous signals that had originated somewhere in this area at irregular intervals and for irregular lengths of time over many years.

The signals had all been on the twenty-one megacycle band and had been detected and triangulated variously by various groups over the years. During the war quite intense efforts had been made to locate the "illegal transmitter," without success. Then peace came and the project had been dropped when someone decided that the signals predated the war sufficiently to indicate an unmilitary aspect and had reinforced the decision by saying that they probably had a natural source.

The matter had rested there until Cal had found the records while digging through University files. Cal was a radio ham, but a political sciences major, and given more to political than scientific thinking, Terry decided wryly. He'd acted as though he thought the signals were part of some tremendous plot, a gambit unnecessary either to the facts or to Terry's immediate interest.

Since the signals were sporadic they were very difficult to locate exactly, especially when adding in the reflections that could occur in mountains such as these. It was, in fact, impossible to triangulate precisely by the normal methods, and it had been Terry's idea to work the triangulation system backward. By using his small portable transmitter, he planned to broadcast prearranged signals from various locations up and down the canyon until he found the exact area that duplicated the original recordings. Cal and some of his friends at Berkeley would be receiving the signals and directing changes.

Terry busied himself with the camp stove, but let most of his attention range in a methodical search of the nearby possibilities for setting up a wire. The bright green cliffs on the far side of the river were practically straight up and down, and there were thin bright shards at the bottom indicating that they were crumbly as well.

It should be quite a challenge to get a signal through from here on the twenty-one megacycle band, though perhaps not if he took advantage of the natural resonance of the canyon itself; but that long antenna would be a neces-

6

sity. Eating with one hand he switched on the regular broadcast band and relaxed, leaning against the camper while it warmed up. His eyes again sought the nearly straight-up green cliffs.

Flipping the now warmed receiver through the broadcast band he was relieved to find that both Salt Lake City and Chicago were coming in with booming signals here, in the daylight. If he could put the wire up just right, those natural resonance effects of the canyon could quite possibly get him very good distance with his miniaturized rig. What a shame, he reflected, that with all the miniaturization of today no one had ever miniaturized a good transmitting wire. In the long run nothing beat the straight, long wire.

Terry caught the faint tracery of a ledge perhaps 120 feet above the river on the far side, and it looked as if there might be easy access. Using the large tree near the camper, a wire stretched straight across the river to that ledge should be just right. By the time he could cross the river and get up there, there should be warm sunlight. If he simply took the transmitter with him, he could set up the station on the far side.

Terry glanced down at the river. Swift current, tumbling between boulders, but not deep, blocked his way. If he were careful he wouldn't even get his feet wet . . . but by the time he'd gotten to the other side he'd discovered that being careful wasn't quite enough to keep himself dry crossing the Feather River.

More than slightly soaked, but triumphant, with the little waterproof field transmitter clipped to his belt· and the wire trailing back to the tree across the river, he had made it to the base of the far cliff.

The cliff, close up, was a crumbling, scaly green, bright but brittle. Climbing it would definitely be dangerous. But the ledge had seemed to descend. Terry made his way up-river, seeking the access, and eventually found it.

The way up was a well-worn but not recently used ascent, clearly a footpath, with haphazardly strewn small boulders that might possibly have been placed as steps for all their irregularity. Terry paused and studied. Yes, they

7

really were clumsily disguised steps. Cliff-climbing for once would be a stroll.

The ledge when he reached it was considerably larger than it had looked, seen from the gorge—a broad, flat expanse, large enough to have accommodated a small cabin; clear despite the green, friable rock that hung from the cliff overhead; and the edge was a sheer drop, a hundred feet, to the river blow.

The bright copper of the antenna wire stretched down in a long catenary loop toward the tree in the canyon below. Sort of an upside down antenna, he decided. Pictures always showed antennas stretching up towards the sky from the transmitting station, but there was no real reason for that except normal usage. This would probably do.

With gaze fixed on the meter, he touched the key. The needle swung over and in the same instant Terry felt the world sway with it.

Earthquake? Terry turned to stare at the cliff behind him, his body tensed to jump from under the inevitable slash of rock.

There was no cliff, no rocks. Instead he was facing a broad marble façade, not so high as the cliff but as perpendicular.

He turned toward the canyon. There was no canyon either—a desert stretched before him, well below the slab of rock on which he stood.

He whirled back to the cliff—to the marble façade. It was there. But—the light was wrong. Greenish. Slowly his eyes traveled up the side of the marble building to the skyline above, to a sickly green sky.

The color of a neon sign, he thought, then automatically corrected himself in a corner of his mind that still seemed to function, though he himself felt numb. It's mercury vapor, not neon, that produces that garish green, the corner of his mind told him.

II

THE FEEL OF THE transmitter key under his fingers brought Terry's gaze back to it, and from there it wandered down the short length of copper antenna wire, now trailing on the ground; only about twenty-five feet of it before it was cut off abruptly.

With a real effort he stifled the impulse to touch the key again. Perhaps it would mean instant return, but perhaps it might bring about any of a dozen other transformations. "Check your premises before you act on them," he seemed to hear Cal's voice saying, an axiom that had brought Terry up abruptly more than once in mutual experimental work.

Terry moved well back from the edge of the slab of stone and turned to survey the building behind him again. Just as he focused fully on it, a crack appeared in the solid gray wall and expanded rapidly in a doorway. The voice that issued from the doorway spoke a strange and unintelligible language, but it was not sufficiently outlandish that Terry could not recognize the basic quality of the sound, the slightly unreal and artificial nature of even the best of electro-acoustical instruments.

"Hello, I guess," he said tentatively, surveying the door without moving.

There was a very brief pause, then the voice spoke up again—somewhat more intelligible this time, though still hollowly artificial. "Grata be you, Citizen Galactica. Thy numero est needful unto me."

Terry stood for a moment in his turn, pondering the evident greeting and request. You might call it English. Archaic, or anyhow approximately archaic English, with a few tags that pointed toward Latin. But the response wanted was obviously a number, so he called off the one that was most immediately in his consciousness: his ham operator's call letters.

Finally the mechanical voice clacked once and sputtered: "Numeros no-numeros. Numeros offered stand not within my ordering, young sire. Prithee, step within yon door. So

9

doing, thou'lt hight a . . . a . . . glowing board, upon which thou'lt place thy right hand. Thy meantime . . . temporary . . . status will be offered thee till this confusion clears."

A plaintive note seemed to creep into the voice after Terry said a cheerful, "All right, if you say so." The volume decreased for all the world (*But what world?* Terry wondered, with a momentary surge of panic) as if the machine were thinking aloud. "So few opportunities to render service in accord with my instructions. Yet beseems that when a service can be rendered the charge is gai unusual. . . ."

Terry advanced somewhat hesitantly through the door. He noted with another, sharper impulse of apprehension that it began closing almost immediately behind him. The "glowing board" of which the coder had spoken stood just to his right as he entered. Though there was a generalized light in the room, the glowing board was the only brightly lighted object visible.

"An it please thee, approach the . . . the scanning panel," urged the voice.

So! It was a scanning panel, now that the machine had located the proper term in English. It was just a solid-looking pane of luminous, milky quartz, or something very like quartz, nearly eighteen inches square.

As he approached it, it rose from its position near the floor to a level appropriate to his own height. A person of another era might have been awed by such phenomena, but Terry was used to various forms of automation, and it didn't startle him. Something new in scanning plates, he thought, recalling one that he had investigated not long ago. That one had been a fiber-optic gadget that had successfully identified his written name sixteen times in a row by cross comparison with a blurred random image printed on the check stubs that went with it.

Terry somewhat diffidently offered his hand to the plate's inspection. Shortly a symbol appeared on the scanning plate, and in the far wall a corridor outlined itself in light. Across the top of the doorway the same symbol appeared simultaneously.

"Subject classed but not identified. Prithee . . . please . . .

10

proceed along left-hand corridor to orientation room displaying symbol."

Terry did as instructed. He wondered at the voice's strange English, yet he felt real admiration for the designer of such a well-functioning device, and he began to have the curious itch that he always called the "take-it-apart" feeling. Any complex mechanism aroused his desire to know the internal structure and operation that produced the results.

He stepped into the "orientation room." It was bare, except for a single piece of furniture: a padded slab which was still adjusting itself to his proper height.

"The citizen is requested to lie prone on the couch."

Terry did so, more out of curiosity than a desire to be obliging, he told himself, as he fought to keep on believing that this was just an elaborate gag. He was immediately aware of a swirl of color that turned into a driving bombardment of all the sensory channels simultaneously. It seemed to go on and on, although in reality he was aware that it ended in a matter of seconds.

"My apologies for the inconvenience." The voice was stiff now, and speaking in a clipped machine-like language which Terry understood. He recognized it as his language. It had searched into its files for the specific type of English he used.

And in the same instant he realized, too, with an almost physical blow of recognition, that this was for real; that there was no longer any possible way he could convince himself otherwise.

Through a sea of conflicting emotions that threatened to overwhelm him, Terry heard the voice continuing. "You have now received a basic orientation as Galactic Citizen. The status of your orientation is and will remain General Citizen until such time as your numeric classification data are located and a more suitable orientation can be arranged. I could not determine your citizenship ratings from the available data in your memory banks since they have obviously been badly scrambled by some traumatic incident. You don't even seem to recall basic galactic symbolism. However, therapy will necessarily be postponed for a more opportune time.

"This is the standard citizen's survival orientation record-

11

ing. You will now please scan the current orientation for familiarity and checking."

Terry forced himself back from the sea of confusion and with an abrupt mental gesture discarded it. If this was real—since this was real, he told himself sternly—he'd better confront it. "You will now please scan . . ." the voice had said, and he wrenched his attention to the problem of just what, and with what tools, he was supposed to "scan," and precisely what was meant by the word "scan," anyhow. To his amazement he found that his own mind was presenting him with an orderly flood of information that seemed to flow on and on.

Surprise was almost immediately replaced with an intense startled interest as he realized that he was now thinking totally in terms of the galactic speech pattern. English, his very own tongue, he could recall perfectly after a slight initial flurry of puzzlement—as if it were a possession he had mislaid on a high shelf. It wasn't where he would have looked for it, and yet it was all there. The difference was that it was now his secondary tongue.

Quite an orientation, he decided. And perhaps the voice —the computer, he noted instantly—was right; that he was a galactic citizen and that some traumatic incident . . .

"*No!*" His whole being surged into the single word that exploded, in English, from his lips. In his brain the new patterns seemed to retreat before the explosion, to coalesce into a separateness, then tentatively to return to the forefront to continue a hesitant, and then more positive presentation of information; and slowly Terry relaxed and again became intent.

There were whole new sets of behavior patterns, strange and familiar at the same time; there were abilities and knowingnesses . . . and that little section marked "survival data"—it came to him with a shock of pleasure that he had learned such odd abilities as staying underwater for twenty minutes (or a very little longer, if necessary) at a time. He gulped. And now his mind was telling him how to regrow—he paused and examined the concept more closely—rebuild was the more apt phrase—any part of his body.

"Yet I'm a whole new me!" he continued his earlier thought, but this time in Galactic. "I'm Terry Ferman, and yet . . ."

"The citizen—Terry Ferman?—has now been restored to the level of competence of Grade One Galactic Citizen, and will realize that the illegal possession of unauthorized electronic gear is detrimental to the general welfare and will therefore report and place into the hands of customs any such gadgetry in his possession."

This demand, Terry realized instantly, was aimed at surrender of the small field transmitter to which he was still clinging.

"It isn't an illegal possession," he returned. "Being an amateur radio operator, authorized by the government of the, United States . . ." He trailed off, overruled by the new information in his own head as much as by the machine.

"No outworld agency can authorize the possession of illegal electronics equipment by a galactic citizen except under off world circumstances. Since you are no longer within the domain of any Terran government, no such authorization may be considered valid."

"But . . . but . . ." The new orientation data was telling him it would be quite useless to argue the point. On some subjects these customs computer sections were quite obdurate, and one such subject was the emission of any type of random or spurious electro-magnetic signal in or near such a computer arrangement. It had not been made clear to him exactly what his transmitter could do, but that its use in this vicinity could quite possibly derange the computer was obvious. And a deranged computer, he realized with a shudder, was nothing he wanted to tackle at this time.

Nonetheless, he clutched the little transmitter closer to him instinctively. It was his last link to his own world. "This is all very well," he said, grinning as he always did when a joke had gone far enough, "but I want to get back to Berkeley."

"The citizen's desire is unclear."

"Don't you understand? I'm lost and I want to stamp my feet on good old *terra firma*, and I want to do it right now!"

There was a pause that was more than a pause. Total

silence set in. A red light went on in the far wall. A wave of fear swept away the momentary homesickness, as the new data in his own head calmly informed him that the next thing that would happen would be a "restraining paralysis for the subject's own good."

"*Psycho!*" said the computer.

"No, no, no," cried Terry. "It's more like, ah, poetry. Look in your Latin banks! *Terra firma* is solid ground. I'm perfectly oriented but I must retain the transmitter. It's the only link I have with the planet I just arrived from. Anyhow, you have no authority to confiscate outworld scientific data or objects from a qualified explorer."

The computer resumed buzzing, busily. And the feeling of imminent disaster disappeared as the red light on the wall blinked off. The silence stretched on and on.

Finally, with the effect of a baffled policeman returning to the real issue, the computer said, "Illegal electronics equipment."

Terry felt his hand tremble a little, but made no reply.

"The citizen is, of course, entitled to the possession and use of standard items of Galactic Citizen's gear, which will be issued on a loan basis by this terminal, since the citizen appears to have lost all the essentials. In addition the citizen will realize that possession of other equipment is dependent upon the classification level of achievement of the citizen as determined by due testing processes. Whenever the citizen can produce evidence to indicate a knowledge of the use and restrictions of use of this instrument within Galactic territory and according to Galactic law, the instrument will be returned. The citizen is now requested to place the electronic device in the slot on the left-hand wall, and follow the directional arrows to the stores area, where new equipment will be issued."

Reluctantly, Terry turned and placed the little transmitter in the slot as directed. He must, he decided, play the game on the computer's terms. It rankled, but the darn thing had all the cards on its side now. The transmitter was not only useless to him on his Quarantine World, but dangerous as well—*Quarantine?* Even as he wondered how he knew

14

he realized how he knew. The orientation had been quite good.

The thought crossed his mind to double talk the computer into returning him, but he rejected the thought. It wouldn't do. Another indication of "psychotic" behavior would result in "restraint for the subject's own good" until a Galactic Supervisor intervened, and, he realized, that might be a long time. There hadn't been anyone of that level here in nearly four hundred galactic years.

With a grin and a shrug he turned to find the arrow trail—and that was when the habit of talking to himself tripped him up. "Just wait until I get a meter on your insides. . . ." he found himself muttering.

He stayed off the silence even as it was falling. "Oh, for Pete's sake," he said, "it's only wishful thinking. Aren't Galactic Citizens allowed to wish? Anyhow, you talk to yourself, too. I heard you."

It was a full second before the intense silence lessened and the light humming of the computer resumed, and Terry realized that any conversation he held, with himself or with the computer, would be taken literally in computer-style and could be as dangerous to him as any possible signal from the little transmitter might have been for the computer. The kind of bantering half-humor that he was used to "thinking aloud" while working would be translated in context and not in intent by the humorless machine and would inevitably cause it to classify him as deranged. He shuddered and made a point of not expressing his next thought aloud.

Well, there was much he now knew that he hadn't known before, and the vistas of unknown information that stretched beyond the brief orientation were dizzying to contemplate. For each bit of data he had received, there were a thousand channels of speculation opening in front of him.

In the meantime, the machine was waiting; not politely, just impassively. He turned again—quietly this time—and followed the arrows away from the orientation room and farther into the huge building.

He now knew the structure was an outpost Galactic receiving station. And he suddenly realized that it was not

15

capable of returning him to his native world, nor did he even know where Earth was in relation to this world. Terry Ferman was a Galactic Citizen, like it or not.

III

THE STORES AREA proved to hold few fascinations. Outside of more suitable light slacks, shirt and sandals to replace his cumbersome cold weather clothing, only five items of equipment were issued. Terry was able to recognize each item from his orientation training.

The first, so far as he could tell, was probably the most useless: a combination translator and personal telephone. It was a small device designed to be worn around the neck, capable of three thousand language sets. It could, theoretically, put him in communication with anyone on the planet. So far as Terry knew, and he knew it with a cold inner certitude, he was the only human being on the planet.

The most useful device in case of danger was a small stunner. It was not standard citizenry equipment but a device issued only on primitive worlds or frontier outposts, capable of rendering unconscious any life form having an electronic nervous system, from human to mobile robot.

Then there was a pair of sunglasses; at least, that's how Terry thought of them. They were capable of a wide range of focus from microscopic to telescopic, and they could also be used simply as glare filters against the bright sunshine that was found on some outpost worlds. But the filter effect was reversible. Quantities of light too dim to see by or of the wrong frequency could be amplified. Cat-eyes, Terry thought, and indeed they were, for even in the total absence of light these lenses could let him see by his own reflected body heat.

A chronograph with a simple numeric read-out face presented a standard Galactic time and local time and included an adjustment rate so that it could be set precisely to the rotation of an individual planet, as well as an indication around the circumference that was graduated to show days, parts of years, and years, all to the base twelve

16

—curiously, the same base twelve system that men used for time, but also curiously different in that the Galactic Standard day seemed to be thirty-six hours in length.

And twelve months to a year, Terry thought, and then realized—not twelve months; not twelve months as he knew them at all. Galactic years—Terry lost himself in computation for a moment. Here the system of comparison broke down. The galactic year was by no means an Earth year; and the twelve parts that one would think of as months of that galactic year were a much longer period of time than an Earth year.

The thirty-six hour day was combined by fives into what one could think of as a week; and there were sixty of these weeks in the galactic month; and twelve galactic months in the galactic year. The galactic year, then, was 3600 galactic days, or 5400 Earth days. The galactic week of five galactic days was a 180-hour week, as compared with the 24-hour day, seven-day week of Earth, which added up to only 168 hours per week. Surprisingly the galactic hour seemed to be quite similar if not the same as the Earth hour, and from there on down the divisions went by 60's, in the same manner as the familiar minutes and seconds back on Earth.

But that five day week? Terry searched back through his memory for an elusive reference. Somewhere, hadn't someone on Earth used a five day week? But the memory eluded him.

He turned the instrument over and was surprised to find three more readings. One puzzled him for a moment until he recognized that the chronograph was also capable of reading latitude on any spherical rotating body. The second reading gave longitude from an original setting; while the third was apparently a compass, giving a reading to tenths of a degree only when the instrument was held stationary. Pretty fancy navigational equipment, he decided. No "lost" Galactic Citizens so long as they had one of these.

The fourth item was a device he knew to be a food converter, although as he thought about it he assessed it as having more the capabilities of a selector than a converter. The operation was simple enough: once keyed by a drop of his own blood, the device would analyze any edible

17

product for conformity with his own diet. It was capable of a limited amount of production of such things as vitamins, and selecting types of proteins and carbohydrates suitable for his diet. It could also refine out poisonous substances or, in case it couldn't fulfill a function, it could state what else was necessary and which types of things were totally impossible. Like the language converter, it had the inherent capability of matching more than three thousand different dietary requirements of as many different life forms. Now it was his, keyed to his needs.

Only five items were to be his out of this storeroom of mysterious treasures. Terry's eyes flickered from shelf to shelf. Then, *Only five!* he thought excitedly. *Wow! Christmases and birthdays all rolled into one! And wouldn't Cal be excited . . .*

With the new possessions strapped firmly about him, Terry left the stores area. The computer, having satisfied its own curiosity—if computers have curiosity, he told himself —seemed to be now leaving him on his own.

His first idea, to explore the building, seemed rather pointless when the orderly new array of information in his head calmly gave him every dimension, every room, every— almost everything he'd need if he were going to build the place, he decided. But one area seemed more promising that the others, and he headed toward the cafeteria.

Passing down a long corridor on his way, Terry suddenly became aware of the emotion-pattern, half-icy curiosity, half-thought that he recognized as snake-thought.

He froze, then turned cautiously and met the reptilian gaze—not of a snake but of something out of such dim past history that he hardly recognized it.

The other being was not large, considering the pictures in museums, nor was he small, considering Terry's only experience with the lizards that he somewhat resembled. About six feet, from head to tail, balanced on powerful hind legs and with shorter forepaws—prehensile hands but not much in the way of arm arrangements.

"A dinosaur!" Terry squeaked, feeling the hairs at the nape of his neck stiffen inadequately.

"A biped!" came in a guttural, dismayed tone from the

18

other in Galactic. Then, "An intelligent biped? Extraordinary!" There was a pause before, gravely and formally, "Grontunk," the creature said carefully. "Galactic Citizen Grontunk," it amplified.

Terry stood unresponsive, gazing at the creature, and a new note entered the other's voice as he continued after a pause.

"Are you perhaps a Supervisor Class? If so, Sir, I wish to register a complaint. I . . ."

"No." Terry found his voice at last, a small voice. "General citizen. Terry Ferman." His orientation was presenting him with several proper patterns of behavior when meeting with a member of another race, patterns that were gradually smoothing out his fight responses. Taking a grip on himself, Terry squelched both sets of reactions—those from his orientation and those from his instincts—and said carefully, "I gather you're not Supervisor Class either? Let's get something to eat and discuss our mutual problems."

Grontunk moved forward, and while one part of Terry's mind was still screaming at him, "Run!" another was coldly analyzing the Saurian's motions; and a third was still informing him that no civilized being had any reason to be afraid of another, so long as both were well-oriented Galactic citizens.

But Grontunk had hesitated, and Terry followed the Saurian's gaze to his own right hand, sweating and extremely slippery on the butt of the stunner.

"I assume that the citizen is not yet fully oriented?" said the growling voice.

With a wry grin, Terry removed his hand from the stunner. "I . . . uh . . . apologize." He paused. "On the . . . world where I have been . . . there used to be some individuals similar to yourself that were classified as somewhat dangerous. I apologize for my instincts. . . ."

Grontunk's tone was only faintly condescending. "Survival instincts are, after all, more a basic than a civilized condition. I, too, was startled by your appearance, though on my home world bipeds have more a nuisance value than danger connotations. Large and carnivorous, they endanger our domestic stock; but I think our hatred and fear of them

19

actually stems from the instinctive revulsion of the cold-blooded for the hot-blooded. However, I am broad-minded and . . ." He trailed off as though flustered and then murmured as an afterthought, "Anyhow, I wasn't too worried about your little stunner. The computer would have cooled you quick enough for irrational behavior."

Terry stared at the huge beast for a full second, his thoughts whirling. And then he felt the reaction setting in: the reaction to all the shifts and changes of thought pattern that had occurred so abruptly and so irresistibly in so short a period of time. The laughter that started, it seemed, at his toes, was as irresistible as the thought-pattern changes had been. He found himself laughing helplessly, while the Saurian stood impassive; though—was that a look of perturbation on his "face"?

The wave of laughter swept through and past Terry, and he patted his stunner once, and got his voice under control. "I . . ." No use apologizing. "You're . . ." he began again, "you're just passing through? If so . . ."

"No." The Saurian started again down the corridor, Terry beside him. "I've been here for nearly five of the local months. Quote awaiting reclassification unquote. Frankly, I thought I was a citizen of the world from which I came, but the computer says I'm a Galactic Citizen so it can't send me back, and for some reason it can't send me on in either. In other words, friend, I'm stuck here and I expect you are, too. Your misfortune is, however, a fortune for me." The growling voice seemed to become gracious. "I was beginning to despair of ever meeting anyone but the computer and Z-9604 for the rest of my natural life."

"Z-9604?" Terry inquired. "Another Galactic Citizen?"

"Only in the broadest possible sense. He is one of the repair robots—servo-mechs. For the computer. Except he's suffered an injury and become disoriented. He now considers himself as an independent—uh, entity. Quite as lost as we are. But without any background-place to wish he was. Therefore he's quite happy. Of course the computer was going to have him repaired, but I pointed out that he could be considered a spare as far as the computer was concerned, and on the basis of Citizen Need I requisitioned him. He

20

makes a better companion than none. But I'm—quite sel-fishly—glad you're arrived."

The problem was beginning to come home to Terry now. They were trapped, he and this cold-blooded Saurian alike; trapped by the inevitable inconsistency of a computer obeying orders literally and blindly. And again it came home to him, the little bit of information that there had been no Galactic Supervisor in this area in nearly four hundred Galactic years.

IV

THE CAFETERIA was a long room with warm light and a cheerful atmosphere that contrasted strongly with the rather cold formality of the computer's rooms, the stores area, and the corridors he'd traversed so far. Perhaps the cheerfulness stemmed from the small tables of all sizes and the "chairs" of odd and various shapes that were scattered about; or from the bright colors in which they were variously painted or upholstered (plastic?); or perhaps from the warmth of the light or the pale yellow of three of the walls. The fourth wall was devoted to food dispensing slots, much like an automat, Terry thought, as he and his huge companion—heavy-built, rather than tall, Terry reminded himself; and perhaps his feeling of its hugeness stemmed from the connotations associated in his mind with dinosaurs—made their way towards it.

Terry searched among strange food-names for some time before he found a section seemingly devoted to his kind of . . . of being, he told himself. The food for which he punched came out after only a short interval, and he turned to find that the Saurian was waiting at a table with chairs that would accommodate both their figures; large, rather heavy chairs, and quite comfortable he found as he sat down.

"So I gather you're trapped, too," Terry began without preliminary. "What have you done about it?"

He was beginning, he noted, to be able to read Grontunk's expressions, and it seemed to him that there was a

21

certain edge of terror, thinly concealed, in Grontunk's reply.

"Nothing. What *can* one do? As a well-oriented Galactic Citizen . . ." The phrase trailed off as Grontunk sat staring, not at Terry but beyond him at an endless future of imprisonment. And Terry's own orientation was telling him that the computer knew best, that his urge toward solving the problem should wait on more competent outside aid.

Without even noticing that he had done so, Terry edited *that* concept out of his head.

"But we can't just sit here! We should at least apply ourselves to the problem of becoming better educated. The concept of better education seems to be tied in with higher Galactic Citizen rating, and would therefore make us more capable of dealing with the problem ourselves."

Grontunk's apathy and detachment were not penetrated. "I have tried, my friend. In order to achieve a higher Galactic Citizen rating, one must, as you say, become better educated. But one cannot become educated beyond one's resources of access to information. And the computer denies access—certain subjects—on the basis of Galactic Citizen rating."

Terry grinned. "Every piece of circular logic draws a line around a blank spot. And where I come from, such a line is known as a zero. Which always has a hole in the middle of it."

Grontunk looked startled.

"If the computer is our problem," Terry continued, "then of course we must reorient the computer."

Grontunk's amazement was succeeded by fear.

"No, no. Without the computer we would die. Neither of us could survive on this planet without it."

"Oh? How's that?"

"Without the computer, or someone else to run it, there would be no power available, no synthesis of food stuffs, no synthesis of breathable atmosphere, and many other things. This world is a desert, lifeless and devoid of the compatible factors that make life possible. You were comfortable when you arrived on the landing stage?" Grontunk

22

looked up at him. "But the air you were breathing came with you. The landing stage appears open, but it isn't. Did you notice the green color of the sky beyond? An unusual color for us oxygen-breathers, is it not?"

"Yes. My home world sky is blue."

"And mine also. But the atmosphere of this planet . . ." Grontunk shuddered. "It is not fit for us."

"Okay. So we're dependent on the computer. But I didn't say that we should destroy it. I said we should reorient it."

Grontunk sank back into apathy, and did not reply.

But, in his own head, Terry heard the answer. "The orientation of the computer is a technical job accomplished only by a Citizen Class . . ." The numbers were meaningless to Terry. "Access to computer orientation controls," the voice went on, "is denied common citizens on the basis of their insufficient knowledge of the techniques involved and the consequences of mis-orientation. . . ."

Another zero, Terry decided. But—if there were a sufficiently serious upset in the computer's operation, it would necessarily call in supervisory help. Now—how serious would that malfunction *have* to be?

Terry wasn't sure. Somehow that didn't seem to be within the realm of a Galactic Citizen's basic knowledge.

"What would happen if the computer had a malfunction?" Terry inquired.

The instant terror on Grontunk's face—odd how he was considering it a face now, despite the saurian features—Terry smoothed over by continuing. "Not a basic malfunction that would threaten our survival, but how serious a malfunction would require supervisory attention? Would make the computer call in Galactic help?"

"I wouldn't know. You must realize, Terry, that we both have approximately the same orientation now. Plus of course whatever our experiences were before we arrived here. My own"—he shrugged in disparagement—"were, to put it mildly, rather limited in Galactic terms. My race, compared to theirs, is not highly advanced." There was a note of chagrin in his voice. "How the computer mistook me for a Galactic Citizen in the first place, I've yet to determine . . . though," in a softer voice, "it has said that I was such a citizen and

23

had a traumatic experience. And I do seem to have absorbed the training rather readily. Perhaps . . ."

"How did you get here?" Terry asked abruptly.

The Saurian seemed to bring himself back to the conversation with an effort. "It was an accident," he said slowly. "At our . . ." There was a pause. ". . . school, laboratory —I'm not sure of the referent—but a place where I was studying. We were investigating . . . those properties of energy . . . I am speaking now from my Galactic Citizen's knowledge rather than from what I knew then—those properties of energy that are of an electrical nature. We had progressed from the point of noticing that friction causes certain objects to attract other objects, to the point where we were producing sparks . . . miniature urgzsplatz." Grontunk paused again. "Lightning bolts would be the term here.

"And I had such a machine in my possession. I was on my way back to the . . . the homeland, you would call it here. And paused in an out-of-the-way place to check over the machinery. More from curiosity than anything else. I cranked up the machine, and then—my world disappeared. I do not yet understand why. My orientation tells me that a signal of some mysterious nature was caused by the urgzsplatz."

Terry had been checking his own knowledge against what Grontunk was saying. Sure enough, there were no referents in basic Galactic training to the equations of electromagnetic energy. A curious blank spot there. So Grontunk had remained uninformed as to the basic nature of his experiment even through the extensive Galactic Citizen's orientation.

There were all sorts of peripheral referents in the orientation to the basic factors of electrical energy equations. The idea of electronic equipment was met with in several contexts; but none of the basics were dealt with here.

"So you created a radio signal?"

"Yes. So I have been told."

"But you don't know why or how? Could you describe your machine? Or do you still have it?"

Grontunk shrugged and quoted. " 'The illegal possession

24

of electronic devices by lower-grade Galactic Citizens . . .'
I had it, but the computer took it away. And told me it
was illogical for a citizen to attempt to contravene measures
based on the welfare of himself and others about him."
Suddenly Grontunk broke down completely and howled,
"But *I* want to go *home!*"

"Home? Where's home?" A well-modulated electronic
voice interrupted and Terry turned to see a glistening metallic individual. "Who is your friend, Friend Grontunk?"

"Oh, hi, Z-9604. Meet our new, uh, meet our new
arrival. Basic Citizen Terry Ferman, this is Independent
Entity Z-9604."

"I greet you most cordially, fellow Entity." The robot
raised both "hands," palms out, in what Terry recognized
as a near-universal symbol of a showing of no-weapons. A
falsity, he realized in the same instant, since a robot of this
class, though not specifically "armed," was quite capable of
bringing force to bear on any opponent it might meet, should
the circumstances call for it.

The Citizen Training, which was now assuming almost a
separate entity-package in his head, began blandly informing him of the capabilities and restrictions of non-specific
robot types such as the one he was dealing with. But
what interested Terry more at the moment was the apparent
coagulation of the Galactic Citizen training itself, and the
separation of his own personality from it. An immunity
reaction? he wondered.

"Perhaps," the robot was saying, "Citizen Terry can inform
me. What is this word 'home' that my friend Grontunk
keeps alluding to? He is a very nice fellow, but he uses
some of the weirdest references on occasion. Myself, I am
an humble entity, but I have intent of understanding that
which I do not."

"Home," Terry replied gravely, "is where the heart is."

"But the heart, in a biochemically housed electronic system, is within the body," the robot answered just as gravely.

"A colloquialism—common to, I gather, all us biochemically housed electronics systems. Perhaps I can translate," he
continued. "Home is that place where a person feels best
oriented, due to familiarity."

25

"Oh. But then *this* is home. Right?" The robot seemed genuinely pleased at having come to a logical conclusion.

"Only for a tin can like you," Terry said.

"How can it be different for me than for anyone else? This isn't logical."

"It is a matter of orientation," Terry explained. "Grontunk's point of orientation—and mine, for that matter—and yours as well—are separated by origin and experience. . . ."

"And therefore," the robot replied, ". . . ah, yes. I see. Orientation is a matter of understanding. Surely any rational being can understand those facts which are presented to him. Therefore home is not where I'm from, but the place about which I have understanding?"

"Yes. Understanding, not just facts." Terry sat staring at the metalloid figure. There were, perhaps, deductions to be made from the basic symmetries of his structure. Bipedal, as he was; and with dextrous upper limbs as both he and Grontunk had. The robot was slightly taller than Terry.

"How much do you weigh?" Terry inquired, and automatically calculated the return answer into pounds. Approximately two hundred. Very close to Terry's own weight. "And how many pounds can you lift?"

But this time he didn't need an answer. The robot was capable of a maximum stress exceeding his own weight by about five times, according to Terry's own information on the subject.

"But you're not made of metal, then?" Terry asked.

"No. Of course not." The robot seemed somewhat surprised. "My metallic appearance serves several useful functions, among which are identification, shielding . . ."

Terry found that he could add the same list himself. The concept of shielding implied without saying so that the robot had an electronic internal organization—and then Terry realized that it implied as well that the tin can must control not only electronic radiation from his own circuits, but his internal heat balance as well. Terry found himself giving way to admiration of the designers of so complex a device, and at the same time wondering who and where they were.

The robot interrupted his thoughts. "Your structure I

26

also find somewhat intriguing. And your designer must have been quite adept, too."

Terry was about to answer this comment when he realized that he had not spoken, and the thought of designers had not been introduced in the conversation.

"Of course not," the robot replied. "I apologize for intruding into your thoughts, but your electronic radiations are so much more intelligible than the sound waves you cause to occur with your—mouth?—that I find them far easier to follow. Your designer seems to have skimped a bit on your shielding quotient."

"If you can read me that well, then the computer can also?" Terry felt himself suddenly as fearful as Grontunk had been.

"Negative." The reply came promptly. "The computer cannot take into account random signals except those received through special channels such as in the orientation room. I, in my turn, am isolated from the computer by a malfunction in my transmitting equipment."

The relief that surged through Terry was so great that he felt sure the tin can could not but register it, but that metalloid entity continued as though not registering.

"It was a game of some success on my part to decode your electrical transmissions. But I must admit that I could only do it from a very close proximity. Of course, such intellectual games one plays for amusement, and I am not completely successful, but then I have insufficient reference points. For example, there was an unusual surge a moment ago which I find totally untranslatable." Terry felt his muscles relax in quick relief, but the robot was continuing, "I also find the name you use for me in these transmissions to be quite intriguing. A metallic food container? Of course, I am neither metallic nor a food container, but . . ."

"I did not mean anything derogatory. . . ." Terry said.

"Of course not. And Tinkan is a much easier form of address than Z-9604. I find the appellation comfortable, and should be delighted if you will use it."

"Good. It's much easier."

"Me too?" asked Grontunk. "It *does* come more quickly to the tongue. . . ."

27

The robot bowed, and Terry asked, "Since you read me, do you read Grontunk as well?" Since the matter was under discussion it would be a good idea to find out as much as possible.

"Only superficially, as in your case. There are many recurrent groupings of electronic responses in your individual computers for which I have no satisfactory referents."

"But if you can receive from us, what is the nature of the difficulty between you and the computer?"

"The signals you emit to your surroundings are of a distinctly different nature than those with which I *should* be communicating with my . . ." There was a distinct pause. ". . . boss? Of course I have a shielding quotient which you seem to lack which would make it impossible, but even without that, our channel of communication would not even follow the same type of code system you use."

A binary system? Terry wondered, and found himself working through a binary numeral computation.

"No, no. That would be a formalized version of your own form of code."

"It is, as far as I know, the simplest possible electronic code," Terry replied. "Does Grontunk also follow it?"

"No."

Terry tried again. There were, of course, innumerable other mathematical codes that could be superimposed on an electronic structure. But the simple form of Aristotelian "yes-no" logic. . . .

"Can be complicated," Tinkan said, "as you say, by innumerable variations. For example, a pulse may be recurrent in time so that the time duration becomes the significant quantity, such as in Grontunk's case. Or a pulse may be present or absent, as in your own case. An individual pulse may also vary in amplitude thus giving what we would call an analogue quantity of informational referent, which is the case of my own basic computational ability."

"But an analogue value can run between zero and infinity. Can you also do decimal computation?"

"I find the value of decimal computation restricted by a large number of decimal points," Tinkan replied, "whereas I can arrive at a much more valid approximate answer

28

with a fewer number of actual manipulations by analogue usage."

"And," Terry replied, "with a great deal less precision."

"But . . ." Tinkan's answer was interrupted by Grontunk.

"If you gentlemen intend to continue a discussion in which I am not oriented, I must either sit here in puzzlement or withdraw. I do not wish to withdraw, for I am beginning to hope that more shall come of this than I had first thought possible."

Tinkan turned to include Grontunk in his next remark. "You have misinformed me. This citizen is obviously not of a Basic rating, since there are no referents available to the Basic Galactic Citizen that would make such a conversation logically possible."

"But he's oriented to the same class I am! And . . . and I don't understand!" Grontunk's voice took a plaintive note. "Without a balancing tail to free his forelimbs, how *could* a biped have developed to a level of intelligence. . . ."

"Both the biochemical and the metalloid forms lend themselves to a variety of shapes," Tinkan interrupted cheerfully. "But, Friend Terry, what is your numeric designation?"

Terry proceeded to supply that which his orientation told him was desired. "Which translates out," he added, "basic citizen orientation."

"Then you cannot know what you just said!"

"That is your opinion," said Terry. "How would you classify me?"

"Sorry," Tinkan answered, "insufficient referents for full classification. But you're definitely *not* just a basic citizen."

"And," Terry replied, "I'm definitely not happy with that classification. Our problem seems to be to refer the matter of status for Grontunk and myself to a Citizen, Supervisor Class, for clarification. In order to get a Citizen, Supervisor Class here, our problem seems to be to create a signal that will call a Citizen Supervisor Class to this outpost. What emergency would cause a Supervisor to be called here?"

Tinkan replied readily. "Why, anything that constitutes an emergency beyond the capability of the computer to inter-

29

pret and handle. Anything falling outside its basic orders would bring about such intervention."

"And how can I get hold of a copy of those orders?"

"That's simple enough. Ask the computer."

"You forget. I'm a Basic Citizen. The computer is not required to give me any information of a technical nature beyond my understanding classification. But I was hoping you might have a copy of the orders."

"Not completely. I do know some of the basics applying to my former job. For example, routine repairs of a predictable nature would be handled by my specific type of entity. However, if the cause of a malfunction is indeterminate so far as the computer is concerned, or if it does not fall within the predictable range of malfunctions, then a Supervisor must be called in to estimate the chances of recurrence and to specifically order any changes required in the computer's routine to prevent future malfunctions."

"Any unpredictable malfunction." Terry sat thoughtfully. Then, "That seems simple enough." He was already rapidly scanning over the general outline of the base and the various functions, not only those that he had been told of, but those that he could, from his own former knowledge, predict.

He had been told that the computer supplied its own power from several units, and that these were automatically monitored and regulated by the computer. But there was nothing in the General Citizen's Orientation to indicate the type of operation factors involved in these units.

"Tinkan, are the power units electrical?"

"Yes."

"Are the power units located close by, within the complex here? Or are they remote?"

"There's a widespread grid of power collection units. They are located most advantageously around the planet, to make use of solar radiant energy, which is converted into electricity for transmission to this area."

"And you have access to the repair department—say, to the switchboard unit that controls these stations?"

"Yes. As a nonspecific technical class I have access to any such in the station."

30

"And if I give you specific instructions, you will obey them?"

"So long as the computer does not countermand your instructions, certainly."

"And you are not in communication with the computer?"

"No. I'm not."

"Then my first instructions are that you bring me a complete schematic diagram of the interconnections and interrelationships of the power collection grid and its termination in this building."

"Such information is not available to . . ." Tinkan paused. "But then you're not, are you? I would have to refer the matter to the computer," he concluded.

"But you are not in communication with the computer. Right?"

"That is correct."

"Then you don't know my classification. Right?"

"That, too, is correct."

"And, in an emergency, your orders read that you will take orders from any rational citizen. Therefore as a rational citizen of indeterminate rank, I order you to bring me this information."

Tinkan sat silent for several minutes.

"You have shown me no emergency factor. And . . . I don't like people pulling rank on me. As an Independent Entity, I must nevertheless follow my basic instructions. Therefore, if you will show me an emergency—"

"Rank, shmank," Terry muttered. "We've got a problem to solve. I'm just trying to make it possible to solve it."

He was thinking fast. There was nothing he could show the robot in the way of an emergency, and it couldn't act as he wanted it to without an emergency. Tinkan had demonstrated he could "feel" logic, probably much the same feeling as Terry had in emotions. So if he could produce an emergency—it would have to be real. An emergency claimed without proof obviously wouldn't be logical—wouldn't work.

Abruptly he stood up, shoving his hands into his pockets to disguise their slight tendency to shake.

"Take me to the power grid control center," he said. "I'll show you that emergency."

31

V

TINKAN SAT BACK WITHOUT MOVING.

"I can take you to the power grid control panel," he said quietly, "but the computer won't let you in. As an unauthorized Basic Citizen . . ."

"Let's go." Terry made his voice firm to cover his nervousness, and Tinkan rose without further comment.

The grid controls were located several floors below, and it took them some time to reach the area, but at last they were facing a door which was inevitably marked: "*Restricted Area. Unauthorized Personnel Forbidden to Enter.*" Terry pushed on the door and found that it did not respond. "Can you open this?" he asked Tinkan.

The robot tried to no avail, and turned. "I, too, am apparently unauthorized here."

"So what does it take to get authorization?" Terry asked.

It was Grontunk who answered, his deep voice a worried growl. "Obviously, orders from the computer."

"And obviously the computer won't issue those orders," Terry decided. "Tinkan, what's the nature of the control operating this door?"

"A simple circuit." Tinkan pointed to a small box holding a magnetic lock closed. "It's keyed to respond only to the proper orders."

"And if it fails?"

"Oh, it's fail-safed. It opens automatically in the event of failure."

"Then we do have the key." Terry felt his hard-held courage slipping, but he reached for his belt and drew forth the small stunner.

"The computer will, of course, notice this action." Tinkan's voice was flat, almost withdrawn.

"But can it identify the action?" Terry asked.

"It will send a repair robot as soon as it gets a failure signal from the door."

"And if we have already passed through?"

"I think," said Tinkan, still in the flat, cold voice, "that

32

it might not notice. But I do not have accurate referents on this."

Terry hesitated a brief second. *If I wait a few days,* he thought, but he saw the weeks growing into months, and the months. . . . Taking a deep breath he aimed and fired.

The door swung silently open, and he was staring at a short corridor that led into a bright room beyond; yet now that the action was taken, now that he had irrevocably set a pattern that unless followed through would create disaster, Terry found himself frozen in inaction, numb, almost not caring.

Grontunk's voice, nearly a whisper, broke into the spell, and Terry shifted his attention from his own feeling of waiting to Grontunk's worries.

"Terry"—the soft, growly voice was hesitant—"perhaps best . . . best we don't all go in at once?"

Terry heard his own voice through the numbness. "Quite right," he was saying as softly. "Perhaps best you return to your quarters now. Then, if anything happens to us . . ."

Grontunk was obviously fighting a battle with himself, shifting uneasily. Then he decided. "No." The voice was still almost a whisper, but positive now. "Alone I have no control over this computer, and insufficient understanding of it to be of any value to you. Therefore, if I wish to escape, best I stay with you. Share the risk to the best of my ability. Lead on, Friend Terry. We Saurians may be ignorant; we are not cowards."

The shocked-surprise part of his mind was coming closer now, watching as Terry listened to Grontunk with . . . with . . . of course! The numbness and the listening were all in the Orientation Entity part of himself.

"Well!" Terry exploded, and then firmly took over his own brain from the patterns of thought that had been so recently superimposed. "Well!" he said more quietly now. Then he turned to Grontunk. "Good decision," he said, "and I gather made from your Saurian instincts rather than your Galactic training, or it would have been otherwise." The numbness was gone from his limbs now, and he started forward, but Tinkan spoke.

"I, too, am undecided," he said. "My former orders and

33

logic tell me that this interference with the computer's operation is wrong. Yet I recognize the problem that you are trying to solve, and the means you are probably planning to use. And, granted the problem, the means is logical. Therefore, if you can assure me that your basic intentions are for the good of a citizen or citizens, and not ultimately detrimental to a larger majority of citizens, I shall continue to assist you."

Terry turned formally to the metalloid being. "As one independent entity to another," he said proudly, "I can assure you that my actions are taken in the interest of the survival of two citizens and are not intended nor planned to be detrimental to the survival of any citizen or entity."

"In that case, my basic commands instruct me to assist you, unless I determine your intent or actions to be otherwise."

"Fair enough. Then let's quit standing around and get inside before the repair robot gets here." Terry entered the door and walked through the short corridor into the bright main control room. "As a repair robot, would you investigate in here if you were repairing a door?"

"Not unless specifically directed by the computer," Tinkan replied. "I would assume that any personnel inside the door were authorized."

"Would your reports to the computer include their presence?"

"No. It would only include the status of operation of the door."

"And would you be able to determine by observing the nerve circuit of the door how its malfunction had occurred?" Terry asked.

"No. Since the malfunction was brought about by an energy discharge that would, as you would say, paralyze or knock out the ability to operate, but would not cause physical destruction of any of the circuits, the malady would be rather hard to determine. I believe I would simply put it back in operation."

"Okay," said Terry, but he felt his muscles tighten as sounds outside indicated the arrival of the repair robot, and

34

in spite of Tinkan's assurances he listened tensely, motioning the others to silence.

The jcb on the door seemed to take forever, though the chronograph on his wrist measured the time as only a few minutes, before the outer door sighed softly shut and cut off further sounds. Terry kept the other two silent a good three minutes longer before he relaxed finally, and looked around at the grid control center.

It was not a large room, but the walls were neatly surrounded by groups of test and control instruments racked into panels, at each of which were seat and desk arrangements, that might be manned comfortably by a humanoid figure. Then Galactics—at least Supervisors—were normally humanoid?

Then the number of the dials and control instruments reached through to him and he began to realize the difficulties of the task he had set himself.

The meters and dials were strangely calibrated in technical units for which he had no referents, since such references were not within the basic citizen's purview. The numerals he could recognize, but the technical abbreviations that went with them would require translation.

Seating himself at one of the panels, Terry began a detailed examination of the board and was amazed to find that since the basic formulas of electronics are balanced equations, he could readily interpret the readings.

Gradually he began unraveling the cross-references from one type of symbol in relation to another, and after a few moments he hesitantly began a series of tests by reaching out and poking buttons, observing responses on the various meters.

Then he moved to the next board, looking for any differences, occasionally asking Tinkan for a full translation of an abbreviated symbol.

Grontunk was standing well back towards the middle of the room, observing everything with wide-eyed curiosity, but not intruding on Terry's concentration by asking questions.

Nearly two hours later, Terry, having examined all the panels in the room, felt that he had determined which was which and which did what.

Most of the panels were identical. They, he decided, would be individual controls for individual stations; while two of the panels were obviously control masters, intended to group the various substations into unified operation, dividing the entire net into two sub-nets.

But he still hadn't determined those distances involved between the various substations, and *that* was important because Terry's plan of attack was necessarily based on the fact that electrical transmission is never instantaneous, and therefore computer-response could not precisely follow alterations in the output of a distant station.

Or could it? Terry wasn't sure, and he would have only one chance to find out.

He turned from the panel he had been examining and observed that Grontunk, as immobilized as a statue, was staring at Tinkan. Then, as his awareness widened to include the presence of two robots in the room, Terry also froze. One of them wasn't Tinkan.

Which was which? Where had the other come from?

But the other was identifying himself by his actions. In turn, he strode to each of the panels that Terry had investigated, scanned the panel, reset an occasional switch that Terry must have left in the wrong position, and withdrew again without so much as a word or any sign of recognition that the room was occupied.

Terry watched the retreating back with a feeling of awe. Had they been noticed or hadn't they? Was the computer even now readying some trap for them? Or, impossibly, somehow still ignorant of their presence here?

Terry noticed that it was only his own icy will that was preventing his legs from carrying him away; preventing a retreat in terror from the unknown.

Shakily he turned to Tinkan. "What was *that* all about?"

"You were no longer seated at the panel. Your presence in a seat indicates that someone is controlling an individual panel, and therefore it need not necessarily remain in prearranged order. But once you leave a panel, unless instructions are to the contrary, computer repair service must necessarily readjust all the manual switches to a neutral position."

"Then the computer knows we're here?"

"Of course not." There seemed to be a slight undulation in the back of Tinkan's voice. Laughter? Terry wondered. "Your presence here is obviously authorized by the fact of your presence here," Tinkan said.

"I get it. Another zero," Terry muttered. "And the computer can only respond to balance an equation."

"Quite right, Friend Terry."

Terry's attention turned again to Grotunk, still frozen in position. "It's all right," he assured the heavy-bodied shivering being. "There's no danger." But Grontunk still stood frozen, as immobilized by instinct as a rock in the forest from which he came.

"Hey!" Terry shouted. "Wake up!"

The Saurian shook in reflex, turned as though to run, then turned back as though having decided that running was hopeless.

"Take it easy." Terry approached the Saurian and gripped him firmly on the almost nonexistent shoulder. "Relax and observe the situation."

But terror was still spreading a blanket over Grontunk's perceptions. "We have threatened it. It will kill us."

"Are you dead?" Terry inquired brutally.

Grontunk came to with a start, and then collapsed into laughter, a peculiar grunting, spasmodic reaction, which was followed by a sudden reflex action in which the powerful Saurian jaws brought gleaming teeth shut with a snap which missed Terry's arm only by his own reflex action.

"Friend Terry, forgive me. My instincts seem to be out of control."

Terry turned to Tinkan. "These manual switches on the panels—the repair robot adjusts them by their positions? By their visible positions?"

"Only if there is a discrepancy that would call a repair robot's attention to the panel in the first place."

"Do we have any tools here?"

With a shock Terry saw Tinkan's midsection open to present a thin interior compartment lined with small hand tools. "Would these help?" the robot asked blithely.

Terry looked at the tools carefully. Tools they were, but not hand tools, except in a specialized sense. They were

37

the equivalent of the replaceable bits that fit an electric drill, or the sockets that fit a special wrench. Terry glanced at Tinkan's hands. Respectably humanoid hands.

"How do you use them?"

Tinkan demonstrated. Finger joints could be slipped out of socket, replaced by special tips. The wrist could be disassembled for heavier power tools.

"Okay. First—put a signal on the wiring system of these chair circuits so that whether we're seated or not it will appear that a Supervisor is seated at each of the nine panels in this half of the room." Terry began directing Tinkan. Time slipped away as they altered the internal workings of first one panel and then another, carefully disconnecting each according to the repair instruction data Tinkan had.

When they had finished, the circuits were reconnected in such a manner that the settings were neutral only with the controls in a wild array of misalignments; which would cause, Terry felt sure, sufficiently unpredictable results to require a supervisor to straighten the mess out.

It remained only for Terry to determine how to reset the manual controls to their formerly neutral positions in such a way that the tampering would not become immediately obvious to the computer.

The supervisor circuit? The one that informed the repair robot whether or not someone was "at" the control panel?

Yes, of course. But how to trigger it?

"Tinkan, these are the large control panels for the power grid. How about the internal distribution system? The one that controls power, say, to the—cafeteria?"

Tinkan led the way through a door into another room. And here were, for the most part, rack after rack of what Terry recognized instantly as circuit breakers, designed to isolate individual circuits in the building.

"The cafeteria?" he asked, and Tinkan pointed out a group of switches on a large panel.

Terry scanned them and was gratified to find that each switch was labeled. One to a machine. Each to a food ordering, maintaining or controlling device.

His gaze fastened on one particular label: *"Fried Stron-*

38

ups Unit." What was a *stronup?* He didn't know, but it sounded like something he himself would never order.

"Grotunk, what the devil is a fried *stronup?*"

"I have never heard of such a thing, my friend."

"Tinkan, is there any way to tell how long it's been since anybody ordered one of these?"

The robot answered promptly. "They're a dish peculiar to a race that has not, in my entire knowledge of the station, been represented by a single member in residence."

"And would therefore constitute an unusual order?" Terry asked.

"I would judge that you are correct, Friend Terry."

"Are there any dry circuits leading from here back to the control panel?"

"Yes. Of course."

"Okay. Then I want a connection made so that if this unit is overloaded the resultant operation of the breaker switch will remove the signal from the supervisor circuit and make it appear that a Supervisor has left each of the control panels that we have just altered."

Tinkan got busy, and Terry began to relax.

"Well, I guess we can go now," he said as Tinkan finished the job.

"But, Terry! What have we accomplished here?" Grontunk asked. "Aside from putting ourselves at hazard?"

"We have, I hope, created a situation in which a Supervisor will be required to intervene." Terry said it calmly, but as they were making their way back to the cafeteria area, doubts began to assail him.

Grontunk knew nothing, or next to nothing at least, of the electrical nature of the universe and therefore could not be expected to understand what they had done. Tinkan also could not be expected to understand the predictable effects of what they had done, since he was programmed primarily to repair existing equipment, and though he would understand to some extent the functions of that equipment, he probably would not take into account the necessary time factors that would influence the results of their changes.

The simple equations for an electronic circuit, especially

39

in a power circuit, almost never include a long-distance time factor—which is necessarily included in a real-life circuit.

Of the three of them, Terry was the only one who understood what effects they could expect to get—and Terry wasn't sure. There'd been no time to make more than rough calculations; to estimate frequencies and transmission times. He could no more than guess at the surge constants of the various lines between the stations.

As they entered the cafeteria, another thought struck Terry. This sabotage was aimed at only half of the power grid; but would that necessarily hold valid? Were there interconnections he didn't know about? Could the computer itself survive the sudden disorienting influence of the loss of half its power? Once he keyed the system, would his next breath be oxygen?—or that pale green gas that seemed to surround the planet?

Firmly Terry suppressed the terror that was creeping upon him.

They had entered the cafeteria, and were clustering about the same table that they'd left. Terry braced his shoulders, but he spoke casually.

"Tinkan," he said, "I have a feeling that the fried *stronups* cooker might be out of order. Would you mind opening the panel so I can check it?"

Tinkan began to oblige, and Terry turned to Grontunk. "We should know soon now whether our effort at sabotage has been successful."

"Sabotage? I do not understand this word."

"A liberal translation from the original French would be," Terry grinned, "to put one's boot in the works."

"But Terry, my friend, would this not destroy the boot?"

"We really don't know yet. But it's usually intended to stop the works. Or at least part of them."

"Friend Terry, I see nothing whatever wrong with the device. Would you care to inspect it?" With astonishment Terry realized that the computational mind of the robot had apparently not made the obvious connection between his current activity and that in which they had been engaged. With a sigh he reached out and took a heavy metallic wrench from Tinkan's belt.

40

"Here's to sabotage," he said, and placed the wrench carefully across the connections that fed power into the device for frying *stronups*.

"Terry! That was deliberate destruction!"

"Sorry, old friend. Clumsy of me. Now put the device back together like a good chap, will you? It isn't harmed, is it?"

Tinkan almost rudely brushed Terry aside and carefully inspected the terminals. "No serious harm. They're merely flash-burned."

Then he began reassembling the unit, and had just completed the job when there was a sudden flicker.

The lights dimmed, brightened and flared, went into a crazy oscillation of brightness and dimness.

Then they were plunged into total darkness.

VII

THE BLACKNESS was nearly complete, but not quite. As Terry's eyes began to adjust he could pick out multiple small spots of greenish glow marking the panels in the room.

Grontunk's voice came to him, loaded with a terror that at first Terry did not understand, and since the Saurian had lapsed into his native language, the words meant nothing to him either.

Reaching for the cat-eyes at his belt which his citizen's training informed him belatedly would be useful under this circumstance, Terry's hand brushed across the translator, and suddenly Grontunk's ravings were being repeated for him in Galactic.

". . . without protection," the Saurian was saying. "The . . . dangerous beasts . . . bipeds . . . may attack. I should never have gotten so far from home."

Terry thought to speak some reassuring words, but as he fitted the cat-eyes lenses over his face, the heat-image picture of the Saurian became visible, hiding under the table, slavering, panic-stricken and, Terry judged, quite dangerous.

Apparently Grontunk was not used to total darkness.

41

"Tinkan," Terry whispered, but was rewarded only by a further scream from Grontunk, "Biped beast! I heard it!" and was alarmed to see the heat-image crouching for a spring in his direction.

"Tinkan! Emergency lights! Quick!"

But there was no response. Tinkan stood silent, the flowing heat-image fading as the body temperature adjusted down toward the background level of the surrounding room, and Terry realized that the robot was not a self-powered unit.

There was a flicker of motion, and he turned back to face the Saurian, charging now, but slightly off balance; charging blind, Terry realized as he stepped behind Tinkan's inert body.

There was a crash, and then a crunch. Grontunk had found something on which to vent his fears—the robot. Terry began to back away.

There was a flicker of light, painfully amplified through the cat-eyes before they responded and adjusted. Some of the luminescent units that lighted the cafeteria came back in operation, and now the scene was ghostly real as though lit by moonlight.

Tinkan and the Saurian were curled together on the floor, neither moving, and Terry was alone.

But no. A twitch, a jerk, each of them began to move. Grontunk looked around bewildered, then asked in perfect Galactic, "What happened?" Slowly he shook himself free of the metalloid body, jerking spasmodically and weakly beside him, and stood. Then, looking down: "Tinkan! My friend! What have I done?"

Tinkan, still on the floor, was covered with gashes and wrinkles, plainly showing toothmarks.

Grontunk looked around bewildered. "I've killed him! But why?" His terror of darkness had receded, Terry observed, but it had left behind a blank incomprehension.

With a more controlled jerk, Tinkan stretched, rolled, stood on his feet, and wobbled erratically.

"What happened?" he asked, but answered the question himself. "Power failure. I must go to my post." He took

42

one step, but as he put his full weight on one massive, mangled leg, it crumpled. Tinkan fell headlong.

And suddenly about them there was the crackling sibilance of a public address system, ill-adjusted to the size of the room, Terry realized, or ill-adjusted to its present quietness. A voice blared out.

"All citizens! Attention all citizens! This station is on emergency power supply. All citizens are required to withdraw to their personal quarters for the duration of the emergency.

"It is further requested that you make an absolute minimum of demands on any power services until the emergency has been corrected.

"Citizens of supervisory rank are instructed to report for duty at supervisory posts.

"Citizens having any knowledge of electronics are likewise requested to put themselves at the disposal of the Supervisors. . . ." Abruptly the voice cut off.

It had been, Terry concluded, a canned announcement. It was now superseded by tones that were more recognizable as the computer speaking.

"Basic Citizens Grontunk and Terry Ferman are required to report to the orientation room. The citizen Murtag is released from detention and is requested to help in the current emergency."

Murtag? Terry wondered. *A new one. No Murtag has been mentioned before.* . . .

Turning, he started toward the orientation room, then turned back. It wouldn't do to leave Tinkan. The speaker system was still humming its "on" signal, and probably worked two ways. "Hey, computer!" he called. "There's a service robot here that . . ."

"The citizen Terry Ferman is required to report immediately to the orientation room. I am aware of the service robot."

Terry felt a chill. Did this mean that he was being put under detention? Restraint for the citizen's own good?

Grontunk had already disappeared down the hall following the computer's command as though he, too, might be a robot. And, Terry inferred, he must also respond to the computer's request or be apprehended.

43

Reluctantly, he turned again toward the hall, and as soon as he began complying with the computer's request, his citizen orientation took over. Reassuringly it informed him, as he made his way to the orientation room, "Basic Citizens Temporary Class must be checked during any emergency to make sure of their stability of orientation."

He was not being arrested, then. A small corner of his mind began to rejoice, and, almost paternalistic, the entity within reached to soothe and reassure. The computer merely wanted to check, and would restrain him only if there were reason to do so. But since he was obviously well-integrated . . .

Somewhere realization dawned on Terry. The computer would be looking not at him, but at the effectiveness of the orientation that he had been given; and that orientation was still complete, still intact, and still under his command. His recent practice in calling it had demonstrated both its intactness and its separateness—and his ability to control it. But for now it was far wiser if it appeared to control him.

"Take over," he said aloud, to that part of himself that was represented in his mind as a small entity, subservient and useful; almost as he would have spoken instructions to Tinkan.

There was a surge of relief from the entity within him. He was obviously rational, it assured him, and therefore need fear nothing from the computer at all.

Almost lightheartedly, Terry entered the orientation room and without being requested stretched out prone upon the couch that had adjusted to his height and contours as he entered.

This time there was no driving, battering of the senses and inflow of data. The flow between the citizen unit in his mind and the computer was rational, well-ordered and brief.

And then a question was addressed vocally to him.

"Your orientation seems to be substantially intact," the computer commented. "Now I relieve you from some of its control to inquire if your prior orientation can be of assistance in my current emergency. I have a lack of super-

44

visors; and you, apparently, have or had some information on the subject of electrical energy." The computer paused. "Under emergency authority . . ." It hesitated. ". . . if the citizen will cooperate, I could grant you temporary assignment to the rank of Technical Assistant. . . ." The computer hesitated again.

"Not unless you're willing to provide me," Terry said firmly, "with a complete course of education dealing with the subject in Galactic Citizen terms."

"Very well."

Suddenly Terry was inundated again with much the same driving forces, the pounding storm of sense impressions that had accompanied his first orientation. But it was brief, and even as it passed, the computer was saying, "The Citizen Technician will now check the orientation, please."

There was a flood of formulas, balanced equations, terms Terry had never met before; and somewhere in its passing he saw and knew in detail the power panels with which he had been working earlier.

"Check. The Citizen Technician will now please report for duty at the power grid control panel."

Terry rose, realizing that he had been in the orientation room a matter of minutes, and was in possession of a better education on the subject of electrical engineering than he could have achieved in a lifetime back home.

On his way to the grid room Terry was passing the cafeteria when two thoughts simultaneously interrupted his concentration on his new knowledge: He was ravenously hungry, and Tinkan was still lying on the floor struggling to reach and repair the damaged to his leg—a repair, Terry realized, that the robot was incapable of performing for himself.

The speaker system was still humming gently, so he spoke aloud to the room in general. "The Citizen Technician," he said, "is in need of sustenance before reporting. And I must have this particular robot fixed *at once*."

"Very well," the computer replied, although Terry's own orientation was informing him that it was pointless to stop

45

in the middle of an emergency to repair a robot when there were plenty more available.

He added, "The Citizen Technician finds this particular robot to be essential to the operation and to the best interests of the station. He is to be left in his former independent condition and instructed to report to me as soon as the recent physical damage is repaired."

Meanwhile, Terry had reached one of the food dispensers, and automatically selected a rather tasteless protein derivative that his stomach and taste buds were telling him he must have. He turned back on his way toward the power grid control center, munching the dry pellets as he went.

The lights flickered on ahead of him and off behind him, in an obvious attempt by the computer to conserve power without hindering his progress. Doors that had formerly flipped open and closed automatically for him either stood wide and unpowered or had to be operated manually. These were little things, but they were indicative of the magnitude of the disaster, and Terry was impressed. This station would probably be hard put to continue operations indefinitely, even with the combined resources of half the power supply and the emergency storage power. But surely a Supervisor would be called now, and Terry's personal problems straightened out . . . ?

Almost instantly Terry realized that this had been wishful thinking on his part. Without power, the station was isolated. Under the present conditions, transporting a Supervisor from one side of the planet to the other by transposer would be a remote possibility, but transporting a Supervisor across a galactic distance would be totally impossible.

Terry wondered how he knew. His orientation wasn't in that field—yet the fields overlapped. He paused for a moment, stunned by the implication. As a technician in one field, his orientation had included references to other fields.

New hope surged. Apparently even the slightest acquaintance with a branch of knowledge was the wedge it took to unbalance the equation of what a citizen could know or be trained to do. . . .

Of course the computer could rely on an off-planet trans-

46

poser, one at the planet from which the Supervisor would come; and energy necessary to send messages could surely be expended.

Yet, if a message had been sent, the Supervisor would now be here—transposition was nearly instantaneous. And, even though there might have been a delay, if a Supervisor were expected, the computer would not have pressed him into service. . . .

There was motion ahead in the corridor, and one of the service robots crossed silently from one compartment to another.

"How soon will my assistant be ready?" Terry inquired of the empty corridor.

"Reactivation is completed. Your . . ." There was a hesitation. ". . . assistant? awaits you in the control room."

With a surge of relief Terry speeded up. A fast repair job. Tinkan would be. . . . But Tinkan was behind him, in the cafeteria! And repairs on that class of robot and to that extent of damage couldn't possibly have been made so fast.

Hope balanced against curiosity as Terry turned and entered the now-open door of the control room.

There were robots here, several of them, standing idly as though afraid to make any move for fear of disaster, but none of them was Tinkan. Briefly Terry wondered how he could tell. They looked alike. Their serial numbers did not show. But, he was sure, not one of them was Tinkan.

Without a second glance at the robots Terry sat down at the control panel which was the main supervisor's link to the half of the grid that was out of operation. The panel itself was dead . . . no. With a start Terry realized that it had simply been turned off. The computer had isolated the cause of the power failure as lying in the control panels themselves and had taken the safest action under the circumstances—turning off those panels.

Terry sat pondering. The problem would be how to get the panels back in operation without letting the computer find out what was wrong. The robots here would be under Terry's orders, but they were also linked to the computer.

As a technician he had nearly forgotten that he already

47

knew what the trouble was; or at least what part of it to correct first. He could go flip a simple switch in the next room and the repair-director circuit that controlled the robots would immediately inform them that there were Supervisors sitting at the panels. But the robots were quite capable of seeing that no such Supervisors were there, and report the anomaly.

"My assistant." Terry looked up at the nearest robot. "Has he arrived yet?"

"Sure. I'm here." A voice spoke from near the door behind him. It was a young voice. It was a soft voice.

Terry turned and stared. The assistant was not a robot.

VII

TERRY SAT, awkwardly twisted, gazing at the newcomer from his position at the main control board.

His assistant was, without doubt, a biped, mammalian variety, young, and female. Decked out in what must be the standard Galactic slacks and shirt with changes appropriate to the female structure.

Terry gulped.

"Who," he asked through a suddenly tight throat, "are you? Where the devil did you come from? Are you . . . ?"

"Student Technician Murtag, Sir. And if you're a Supervisor Class. . . ."

"No."

The bright face fell, the eyes turned away. "Damn," she muttered. Then she turned back, a flare of anger sparkling in her eyes. "*When* are they going to send a Supervisor? How long must I continue to battle with this imbecilic batch of wires and resistors and . . ."

One of the robots spoke up. "If the Citizen is not yet feeling stable. . . ."

Fear chased the anger from her face.

"No, no. I'm all right." She turned again to Terry. "I'm at your service, Sir," she said as formally as though she herself had turned into a robot. "I understand there has been an emergency?"

48

Terry was thinking furiously. The girl was obviously as defiant of the computer as she was terrified of it and, by implication, the computer was probably alarmed by the girl. He'd better force her to take control of her emotions before the two fears clashed with inevitable consequences to her.

"If you have personal problems," he said, forcing a coldness he did not feel into his voice, "we can, perhaps, discuss them at some other time. Our immediate problem is to find the cause of the power-system failure, and to amend the damages if possible."

There was a slight rebellious quirk in the girl's gaze.

"And I might point out," Terry continued, still in the cold, formal voice, "that it will not be a matter of stasis only"—here he had leaped intuitively to a conclusion—"but a matter of life and death to see to it that the units are—put back in operation."

Terry knew himself for a liar even as he spoke, but the speech was directed as much to the computer as to the girl. His own survival as well as hers, outside a stasis chamber, depended on whether the computer considered him a reliable, able citizen or—not quite an enemy, but a threat to the computer's stability in carrying out its own functions and orders as it interpreted them.

As he finished speaking, another robot came in from the corridor, and Terry felt a lurch of gratitude, of relief.

Tinkan was back.

How did he know? Terry wasn't sure. A hunch? A feeling?

"Tinkan?" he asked.

The robot bowed. "Independent Entity Tinkan, reporting for duty. I see you've changed status."

The other robots stood impassively, and Terry turned to them.

"Your presence here," he said bluntly, "is no longer required. These two will be all the assistants I need." And to the humming speaker system, "You can save the speaker juice now, Computer. I want to concentrate and the humming bothers me." Abruptly the humming stopped, and the robots turned as though a single unit, and marched

49

back through the door leading to their quarters. Involuntarily Terry shuddered. Quarters where they might stand a thousand years, or from which they might emerge in moments, depending on whether situations called for them.

"Okay, Tinkan. Let's return . . ." Terry paused. First, he decided, he must make sure that it really was Tinkan. But how?

Tinkan? he thought, concentrating.

Nothing happened. Maybe he'd been mistaken? But he'd been so *sure*. Then he remembered Tinkan's words and forced them into full recall to hear them exactly. ". . . *decode your electrical transmissions . . . only . . . from a very close proximity. . . .*"

"Tinkan," he said aloud this time, "come here."

"Yes, Boss."

Boss? Terry wondered. *Now how the devil did I get that title?*

"Well, you've had a raise in grade," Tinkan answered the thought from beside the console, "and I'm under your orders now."

"Okay," Terry decided. "You're you." Then he turned to the girl, standing as silent as one of the servo-robots, and awaiting orders which he knew she would try to obey with robot-like precision; but also radiating a defiant air which indicated a free being forced to do something by powers beyond its will.

"Relax," he told her. "The computer's not monitoring this room right now. And while we have the chance I want a brief rundown on your history. But first"—he turned back to Tinkan—"put those panels back the way they were, including the switch in the other room. Can you do that without help?"

"Sure, Boss." Tinkan was halfway out of the room before he finished speaking.

"Now." Terry turned back toward the girl, his voice brusque to hide his pleasure in finding her here. She was staring at him in wonder.

"Who are you, private controller of robots? No citizen below Supervisor's rank is capable of that. . . ." She waved her hand vaguely toward the door through which Tinkan

50

had disappeared. "But you're not a Supervisor. Who *are* you?"

"Terry. Terry Ferman. At your service, Ma'am." Terry made a low bow, but the girl was unimpressed.

"Are you a pirate?"

"Not to my knowledge."

"Your reference to the panels . . . you spoke as though something had been done to them. Yet you told me that there'd been an accident. There had been damage."

Tinkan had returned and was proceeding to remove panels and change circuits beneath them. Suddenly the girl gasped and the hostility fled from her face.

"You've done it! You've managed to take control of the computer! I tried that myself, but it put me in stasis." Then a puzzled look came over her face. "Time. What time is it? And where did you come from? You can't have been here before, or I would have known."

"Before when?" Terry inquired.

"Before I was put in stasis. Just a little while ago." The date trembled on her lips, and Terry felt cold. Three hundred and seventy-three galactic years, he translated silently.

"That explains why you didn't know I was here." He glanced at the wall where the read-out panel flicked over seconds, minutes and hours, days and years. "Hadn't you noticed the date?" he asked gently.

The girl stared at it, but seemed not to comprehend. "But it was only a few minutes . . ."

"Apparently the computer thought you were an enemy."

The girl's composure broke. "I was only trying to get home!"

"Home?" Terry asked.

"Yes, Sir."

"Home is where the heart is." The voice came from the robot, and he spoke without looking up from the wiring he was doing. At his voice the girl shrank back.

"He's okay," Terry said. "Free Entity. Not under computer control."

But the girl shrank in further terror. "An uncontrolled robot!"

51

Tinkan looked up. "Nonsense," he said. "I haven't eaten any maidens in the last three thousand years."

"Who said anything about eating maidens?" Terry asked.

"She did." Tinkan pointed a finger tipped with a soldering iron.

Suddenly the girl regained her composure. "I said nothing of the sort. And I direct you . . ."

"Countermanded!" Terry spoke fiercely and abruptly, sensing, guessing rather than knowing, what the girl had been about to say. "Tinkan receives orders from no one but me. Understand?"

"But an uncontrolled robot should . . ." The girl gazed at him speculatively. "But no, of course you're right. I see. The old rules no longer hold, do they?"

Terry was about to ask further questions, but the girl was staring at him, still speculatively.

"And of course the old rules don't apply to you, either, do they? Being out of category doesn't necessarily imply that you're a . . . criminal?"

Terry said, "I gather the computer has you similarly classified?"

The girl shuddered, and said forcefully, "But I'm not! I'm really well oriented!"

"What's your classification?" he asked abruptly.

"Student."

"And you were in transit?"

"There was an emergency. Our school thought it best that the students all return home. But when I got here the computer didn't send me on. It said it had to wait for an 'opening.' What should have taken me only minutes stretched out into hours. Finally I began trying to get a message through, to get someone from back home—anything to get out of here. But the computer wasn't sending the messages. It kept saying it had to wait for an 'opening'—whatever it meant by that. Then . . . then I said I'd send a message myself, and it said I was being irrational. I got angry, because *it* was the one being irrational. I had to get home!" She said it defiantly.

"And then you did something the computer didn't like?" Terry asked gently.

She grinned—a gamin grin. "I forced my way into the comm center. I made it think I was a Supervisor. But when I tried to send a message, I . . . I guess I tuned the dial wrong or something. There was a sort of splatt, and then a robot came in and I guess I was pretty furious. I took a tool from a rack and I . . . well, I threw it at the robot. But there were others, and I got scared. I . . . there's a big switch near the message desk and I pulled that. A lot of the lights went out, and I ran and ran—but there must have been some power left because a robot stopped me, and . . . well, that was . . . I mean . . ." She glanced again at the chronometer complex on the wall. "I guess that was a long time ago," she ended in a small voice.

Terry was scanning his own orientation. The computer, he was informed, even one such as that controlling this area, was not allowed to hold a citizen without informing superiors so that the matter could be quickly resolved. Obviously, something was very wrong here. A Supervisor should have been called the minute the girl was put into custody.

But the last Supervisor in this area had preceded the girl's passage by nearly twenty Galactic years.

The computer, then, had failed in a basic responsibility. Involuntarily, Terry shuddered. That machinery could fail, he knew—as Terry. But that a computer could fail in so basic a matter was incomprehensible; totally out of agreement with anything he knew as a Galactic Citizen.

"You lived on one of the out-worlds?" he asked, a new thought striking him.

"No. But there was a transportation problem. It seems a great many people were responding to the emergency. I couldn't get a direct route home. They explained to me, back at the university, that the route I was taking was unusual, but necessary in the public interest."

"Had that ever happened before?" Terry asked.

"No. Oh, no. Not ever. At least not in any of the history books I've read. Transposers don't fail, and you can go any- where whenever you please. I was surprised when they said I couldn't take a direct route, but when they said 'public interest,' of course I didn't ask any questions. But

53

always, the longest distance is only three transpositions at the most. Why, only last month . . ." Her voice hesitated. "That is only a month before . . ." She stumbled and went on. "I visited friends almost across the galaxy, in three . . . three . . . but they're probably . . . dead now? Three hundred and seventy-three standard years? And . . . my family?" Horror turned her soft young face rigid for a moment, and then the tears began to come. Terry reached out a comforting arm, then drew it back. He couldn't intrude. Helpless, he watched her cry, great choking sobs that shook her slender body, and doubled her half over.

It was stormy but brief, to Terry's surprise and relief. In one gesture she choked off the sobs, threw back her head and glared at him, then turned her back, probably to regain her composure, he thought.

Tinkan's voice, flat, uninflected, came as a welcome interruption. "Okay, Boss. The circuits are all back in order."

"All right," he said gruffly. "Let's get down to the actual business of finding out what damage has been done. You start on that station over there." He glanced up and saw the girl, recovered but still white. "Uh, Murtag . . . er . . . well, for gosh sakes, haven't you got a better name than that?"

"What's the matter with my name?" the girl flared. Then she quieted. "My friends call me Pietra. If you'd like to use it . . ."

"Piet." Terry shortened it immediately. "It fits the tongue better. I will use that.

"You start on that panel over there," he said.

The girl retreated toward the indicated board, and Terry turned to the master panel. Hooking it back into the circuit, he began flipping the switches that would turn on the test functions of the various panels.

The routine test patterns and checking seemed to fall quite naturally into a category of familiarity that would have astounded him if he had thought about it.

Of the eighteen stations supplying power to this sector of the grid, nine were now totally inoperative; the others were apparently unhurt, or on standby, and could be keyed back in to immediate operation.

Suddenly Terry seemed to step back and view himself from a distance. His "now-trained-gaze," his orientation pattern, proceeded almost as a robot without his supervision, and he stood back watching it in awe.

The story that was unfolding from the meters and dials was the story of a disaster that he had created; but the orientation seemed unaware of that. It was deducing the cataclysmic shock waves that had swept the grid. It was seeing in detail the results. But it was finding the causes thereof unfathomable.

And Terry realized that the orientation was a complete package. There were facts it didn't have. He could relax. That something had happened would be known both to his orientation and to the computer that had supplied it; but it would not be known that he was the agent of that something. No amount of tracing the faults shown by the record could show precisely how the shock wave had originated; how the loss of synchronization had occurred. Only what the results had been.

There were no records to tie the two together—his action with the action of the grid.

He was assured now that the nine stations that were unhurt could be keyed back into the overall pattern safely, and mindful of the tremendous drain that was being put on the emergency reserves by the eighteen inoperative units, he keyed back in the nine operable stations.

Only one of the remaining stations had been seriously harmed. The others could be repaired readily with the available stockpile of materials on the planet. But this one would require off-planet resources.

Not a very serious matter, Terry decided, since it represented a good deal less than one-thirty-second of the available power resources, but it would be interesting to find out what the computer did about it. Apparently there was a jam-up in off-planet communications, *reasons for* and *extent of* unknown. The computer's basic orders would demand that the station be fixed.

What did the computer consider to be a matter of comparable magnitude that would prevent its action in this direction, as it had prevented the calling of a Supervisor when Murtag was first restrained? Or when Grontunk, or he himself, arrived?

Terry felt sure that there would be no off-planet communications. He lacked data to know why, but the fact was obvious. Would this be a malfunction in the computer itself? Or from some other cause?

"Will there be anything else, Sir?" Murtag's voice was gently inquisitive, as though not wishing to interrupt.

Terry came to with a start.

"No. I guess that's all. We've done our job here for now. As the repair crews operate, of course, we will have to—supervise the cutting in of the repaired stations. End of emergency. Work crews dismissed," he said.

And then he grinned. "Let's go see about getting something to eat," he said.

Murtag smiled shyly, but she said teasingly, "Is it proper? Consorting with the boss, I mean? During off-duty hours?"

"Well"—Terry's tone matched her own—"that's more or less up to you, but you might find it a little difficult to consort with anyone else. So far as I know there's only one other citizen on the entire post."

There was a barking cough from the hall. "He means me," Grontunk's deep voice interrupted. "I obtained permission from the computer," he added, "to watch through the door. I implied that it would help my stability rating to know that there were other citizens around. And"—there was a bubble of excitement in his voice as he continued—"it finally agreed to grant me student rights. I'm not sure, but I think I've won something!"

Terry laughed. "Yes, I guess you have," and they all headed along the corridor toward the cafeteria, Tinkan bringing up the rear.

As they were entering the cafeteria, Terry turned back toward Tinkan. "Why so silent, my friend? I don't recall your having said anything now for hours."

"As a servo-mechanism"—the voice was flat and logical—"I respond when spoken to."

"But you're not a machine. You're an independent entity."

"Are you canceling your orders, Boss?"

"What orders?" Terry was puzzled.

"You ordered that I was to take orders from no one but you. That, logically, takes me out of the category Independent Entity and places me in the category servo-mechanism."

Terry stared in surprise, then in dismay, at the robot. Was freedom something that a more responsible being could take away, so easily, from a lesser?

He glanced around to see both Grontunk and Murtag stopped a short distance ahead, and apparently waiting for his answer.

"How about it, Murtag?" he asked. "Can you accept Tinkan here as an equal and a friend?"

There was a long pause. "It would be very difficult, Terry. Where I come from, a robot is a machine that keeps its place."

"Grontunk?" Terry turned to address the Saurian.

"No problem here. Where I come from we don't have robots, and Tinkan was my only friend here for some time."

Terry turned back to Murtag. "Because Tinkan is, and could behave, as an Independent Entity—*you* are out of stasis." His voice was fierce with a furious intent. "And," he added, "because of Tinkan we have a chance to solve the problem here. And," he continued after only the slightest of pauses, and still with the fierce intent of fury in his voice, "you will treat him not just as an independent entity, independent of a controlling computer, but as a *free* being and an equal. Whether you accept him as a friend—and only that factor—is up to you." Angrily he turned and strode to a table.

There were footsteps behind him. "Terry—Terry. Don't be angry. I . . . I didn't know, and I'm not asking how. And I'll try. But don't be angry!"

Terry looked back, and saw that Tinkan had not moved. "Tinkan?"

"Yes, Boss." It was still a flat, machine-like tone.

"I give you one suggestion, which you may refuse if you like: to accept the responsibilities of a free individual to the best of your ability, and to accept no further orders

57

from anyone, other than those that you accept of your own free will."

He paused and looked into the immobile features of the robot. "If you accept," he said, "you are free."

The robot stood silent and impassive. There was a shadow of fear on the girl's face, and Grontunk's Saurian features were immobile and unreadable. Perhaps he had undertaken too much, Terry was beginning to think.

Then the robot moved, bowed low, and said, "I accept. Thank you, Terry. I will do as much for you some day."

VIII

THE LITTLE GROUP had been gathered around the table in the cafeteria for several hours, becoming better acquainted and coming more and more to realize that they had won a minor victory. But the thought kept nagging at Terry that the victory had been hollow. They still had no complete understanding of the problem before them. The computer had demonstrated erratic behavior, yet they must trust it.

Terry turned to Murtag. "There was an emergency that brought you here. Do you know what kind?"

"No, Terry. They didn't say. I gathered it was serious. But nobody ever said what it was."

"A war?" Terry asked.

The girl frowned. "I would find that hard to imagine. There were always minor squabbles, but there hasn't—hadn't been a major conflict in centuries."

Terry turned off that track, unwilling to badger the girl for information she obviously didn't have. But where else could he look?

His gaze fell on Tinkan. "You were around then. Do you have any idea what that emergency was?"

Tinkan shook his head in an almost human gesture. "I was a repair robot then. Nobody ever bothered to tell me anything but to fix this and fix that. I noticed Murtag's arrival"—Terry felt rather than saw Murtag flinch at the mention of her arrival, but she seemed to relax as the robot

58

continued—"but it meant nothing to me. Shortly after she got here she asked me for an item that was unavailable and seemed surprised when I told her we couldn't order it from Interplanetary Stores. She said that didn't make sense. Of course, three hundred and seventy-three years ago she'd have been right."

"Had the computer given you any reason why you couldn't order from Interplanetary Stores?"

The robot seemed slighly embarrassed, and answered obliquely, "Does your left toe ask why you step on it?"

"Okay. So we're cut off here." Terry was speaking as much to himself as to anyone else. "It's up to us to find out why. I find nothing in my own experience on which to base a conclusion. I can't see *why* we're trapped. Can any of you?"

"I can't even see why you think we're trapped," Tinkan answered. "We have a complete environment. We are not restricted. Most of our needs are met. And we're well oriented. You said yourself, Friend Terry, that home is that place to which you are best oriented."

Terry was about to reply when Murtag answered for him. "You're wrong. Here our freedom is limited. The confines of this"—her hands made a gesture—"this base. We *must* get out. We must find out. . . ." Suddenly she burst into tears. "I want to go home!" she cried. "Even if my family *is* gone. Even if everything *is* all changed. I want to go home!"

"It's still a matter of orientation," Tinkan decided, unimpressed by the tearful outburst, "but I see that you are faced with an unresolved problem."

"Take it easy, Murtag." Terry reached over to touch the girl's shoulder and her sobs subsided a little.

Searching for a quick way to change the conversation, Terry turned to Grontunk. "You say the computer made you a student observer?"

"Yes. It seemed to have decided that my orientation was not quite stable, and I was looking around for some method to keep it from cooling me. So I began talking about how I couldn't be expected to be stable if I weren't also useful. When it pointed out that I couldn't be useful without knowing what I was doing, I argued that I couldn't

59

very well know what I was doing until I had learned something. It agreed that I could learn, by observation, and intimated that this was a prerequisite before it could give me any orientation on the subject."

"Oh?" Terry was startled. "How about that, Murtag? You were a student. But the computer is quite capable, apparently, of training anyone to any level of knowledge within its limits. You know, the orientation things," Terry said.

"Oh. Yes. But they're only like reading books," Terry said. "They're only a set of knowledges."

"Hunh?" Terry was taken aback at the concept. The orientations he had experienced were quite different from his concept of books, including as they did complete programs of action coupled with wide scopes of knowledge. "But a person could learn anything from. . . ."

"Sure," Murtag interrupted, "and when you got through, you'd be just like any servo-robot—fully pre-programmed, but with no real basis for independent judgment and operation. Actually," she continued soberly, "it's more dangerous than that. The orientation impresses sets of facts and available action patterns on . . . unused portions of your mind, facts and action programs available for your use. If *you* use *them,* fine. But if they're beyond your comprehension, they're apt to act as the strongest part of your mind, and . . . well, that's the pre-programmed servo-effect. The oriented facts and actions part of your mind dominates, and there's no *you* left, no judgment, and no independent operation."

"Oh." That agreed with what he knew. "Then what is the normal process of learning?"

"Observation, usage of the facts and actions available, and deduction. At the University with each set of facts and patterns you were given, you were required to exercise them until you had advanced the concepts contained in those facts and had deduced what the next set of facts should be. Of course the training program included orientation, but without using the orientation to the point where you had gone beyond what you had been given . . . well, it just wouldn't work."

"I don't quite see that," Terry said. "It didn't take the

60

computer but a few minutes to turn me into a competent electrical engineer."

"Yes, Terry. But, with the same knowledge it gave you available to it, the computer still couldn't do the job itself. And you *have* had experience with and made deductions about electrical engineering, haven't you?"

"And Terry," Tinkan interrupted, "you had already deduced enough of the operation of this complex to throw it very competently out of order, and without leaving any clues as to the methods by which it was thrown out of order. May I say that those deductions were several orders of magnitude greater than those required for the training—the orientation—that you received?"

"But," Terry insisted, "the computer couldn't know that. Or could it?" He found himself trying to quiet an unreasonable fear that had risen at Tinkan's words. Could it? he wondered.

"If it had," Murtag was saying, "you would have been in stasis real quick. Yet the computer knew, somehow, that you were capable of utilizing the training in electrical engineering, and making value judgments that it could not make."

"Then," Terry said slowly, "actually . . . from that we can deduce one of the laws of the operation of the computer. It is programmed to respect human value judgment above its own."

But Murtag was shaking her head. "Not so, Terry. If that were the case it couldn't cool anybody for anything."

"Okay." There was a long pause as Terry considered this one. "The computer, then, must have a value judgment of its own about the value judgment capacity of citizens. This would necessarily imply that the computer is capable of comparing something with something to form a value judgment which it can apply to individuals."

"Ability demonstrated by action," Murtag said. "Did the computer test you?"

Terry frowned. "I'm not sure. What do you mean by test?" He began searching for the answer himself. It would have been in the orientation room. He concentrated on seeing that room around him, on hearing the sounds, and . . .

61

there it was, the computer's voice: *"Your orientation unit seems to be substantially intact,"* the computer was saying. *"But I relieve you from some of its control. . . ."* (Control? Yes. Basic Citizen's Survival Orientation would contain a control factor, which could, but need not, be overcome, depending on the ability of the citizen to survive without it. That made some sort of sense, he decided.) *". . . to inquire if your prior abilities can be of assistance in my current emergency. I have a lack of Supervisors. And you apparently have or had information on the subject of electrical energy. Under emergency authority . . . if the citizen will cooperate . . . I could grant you temporary assignment to the rank of Technical Assistant. . . ."*

That, Terry realized, had been the test question. But the scene was still progressing.

"Not unless you're willing to provide me"—Terry heard his own voice replying—*"with a complete course of education dealing with the subject, in Galactic Citizen terms."*

And *that* had been the rational answer, rational in the computer's viewpoint, that had caused the computer to give him the technician orientation rather than that of assistant technician.

The computer would judge by that answer that he *did* know electrical theory, but must be given a coherent set of facts to apply it in this area.

"Yes," he said slowly, "I was tested, but I didn't recognize it at the time as a test. It asked me if I knew electrical engineering and would help it. I said sure, if it would give me the facts in Galactic terms. I see that there are several points the computer could deduce from this answer. First, a confidence in my own ability; second, an understanding of its problem; third, a willingness to apply my ability to a solution of its problems; and fourth, a rational attitude toward my own limitation, that of not having learned electronics in Galactic terms,"

Then he went on. "Now it's our turn. We've got to formulate a question for the computer to find out why it is refusing to respond in a rational manner in failing to call supervisory help. We have some partial answers on hand. The computer knows it needs help; otherwise it wouldn't

62

have advanced me in grade without further authority. So—either the computer can't get any other help; or—it's forbidden to do so by factors of which we are not aware."

Abruptly another recall scene came into Terry's awareness. It was Tinkan speaking this time, out of the past: "... *predictable range of malfunction ... to estimate the chances of recurrence and specifically order any changes required...*"

"Part of my job," he said aloud, "as highest ranking electrician here, will be to order any specific changes in the computer's operation that might avoid a future malfunction of the power grid. That means that I could specifically order that a Supervisor be called." But even as he was saying it, Terry realized more, and added, "That wouldn't work. The computer obviously *can't* order a Supervisor in, for some reason as yet unspecified."

He frowned deeply. "Murtag, is it usual practice for a computer to requisition and reorient citizens?"

"Within emergency limits, yes."

"Then the computer considers itself to be on an emergency basis, and has since we arrived."

"How do you deduce that, Terry?" The Saurian's voice growled with interest, and Terry was amused to hear the student-attitude even in that incongruous articulation. Grontunk was so busy trying to live up to his concept "student" that he was forgetting to be scared. Just as well.

"It's obvious. Every action we know of that the computer has taken in the last three hundred and seventy-three Galactic years"—Terry brutally underscored the time factor—"has been irrational except as it might be excused by an emergency situation. We can also deduce a malfunction and long-term memory lapse on the part of the Galactic Civilization since, obviously, it has not gotten in touch with this outpost in that time—perhaps like Rome, a civilization on my planet that collapsed and forget its outposts in Britain, it has simply forgotten that this post exists."

Terry, remembering the history of the Roman legions in Britain, suddenly shuddered. The collapse of the Roman empire, on the planet Earth, had been a comparatively recent event—compared to whatever had occurred here; for

63

Rome had forgotten Britain only one hundred and eleven Galactic years ago; and during that comparatively short span of Galactic years, Earth itself had grown a civilization that had engulfed both the fallen empire and its forgotten outposts. The situation, then, that had affected the Galactic civilization had been greater, more thorough, than that which had torn Rome asunder and made her easy prey to the Huns.

There was a memory connected with the relinquishing of his little transister rig—how long ago? It seemed forever. He reached back for a recall on the incident . . . and the computer was saying ". . . *produce evidence to indicate a knowledge of the use and restrictions of use. . . .*"

"That's it!" Terry felt a growing excitement. "We can solve the problem by becoming Supervisors! The computer has indicated its own knowledge of a lack of them, and has shown a willingness to create them. We've got to become Supervisors."

"But, Terry—" The girl was frowning. "It takes years to become a Supervisor. And the computer can't possibly train you to that status."

"Oh?" Terry sat back and was about to continue, but there was a set of information being presented to him from the Citizen's Survival Unit (as he had finally decided to call his first orientation). The word "Supervisor" didn't translate out quite as he had been using it; it didn't mean a person designated to control. The concept was more that of a free-willed individual with a sufficiently broad understanding of enough areas of knowledge to be able to exert competent control.

But that, too, he realized, was not complete. The missing factor? Experience. Not just knowledge, but experience in forming value judgments based on knowledge.

Again, he was back in the orientation room, realizing the infinite possibilities opened out by his first orientation.

"What percentage," he asked suddenly, "of students such as yourself became Supervisors?"

"It varied." The girl looked at him speculatively. "There are very few people," she continued, "with the necessary drive to accomplish so much in integrated training and experience, and who will accept the rank of Supervisor as a sufficient goal unto itself."

"Pardon me," Tinkan's voice interrupted, "but I personally find the goal of achieving responsibility to be a very good one. That's what freedom is, isn't it? And with the expansion of responsibility comes expansion of freedom. I find it extremely logical."

Terry found himself wondering how deep the robot's resources really were. Could Tinkan expand his responsibility? Or was he merely a mechanical parrot?

"I think perhaps I can expand somewhat, Friend Terry," said the metallic voice. "I have already begun wondering how to extend my freedom by becoming less dependent on the main power source. Recent events have shown me that such dependence precludes to some extent the freedom I seek; and precludes as well the possibility of my performing such responsible actions as I might wish, to demand of myself under emergency conditions."

"Well, that at least is something that we can do something about, and would seem to me to be a worthwhile effort to make." Terry was gazing at the robot now. "We'll have to figure out how you're connected to the power supply, and what your power requirements are, but it shouldn't be too difficult to work something out. It occurred to me, during the recent emergency, to wonder if the apparent design deficiency . . ."

Murtag broke in. "It's not a design deficiency, Terry. If you will consult your basic orientation you'll find that robots are deliberately restricted. During emergency circumstances the possibility of erratic behavior was thought by the original designers to be a sufficient problem to warrant a fail-safe connection. You must realize that even the computer would have been temporarily knocked out by a sudden change in the power supply."

"But that consideration definitely wouldn't apply to Tinkan, since, if he's not connected to the computer, he wouldn't get any erratic orders from it in case of a power failure. But wait a minute, any life form that operates with an internal computer—and that means us, too, of course—can be knocked out by a sudden change in the power supply func-

65

tion. That *would* be a safety mechanism, wouldn't it? Something we'll have to take into account in changing Tinkan's connections."

"Okay," Murtag agreed somewhat hesitantly. "I believe I begin to see some valid reasons behind your idea of free robots." She shuddered involuntarily. "Though I admit the concept to be completely foreign to my former thinking."

Terry noticed that Grontunk had quietly gone to sleep in the middle of a sentence. The Saurian's snores were something awful to hear, and Terry realized that he, too, was in need of sleep.

Murtag was uncomfortably curled up in the tiny chair, and finally gave up fighting her heavy eyelids, and she fell quietly asleep.

"I find need to withdraw for computation, and suggest that you do likewise," Tinkan said.

Terry rose and stretched and made his way to his own quarters, leaving the other two to sleep as they would.

As he was dozing off, Terry seemed to hear a voice in the distance.

"The Earthling," it said, "shows more promise than any we have dealt with recently. Perhaps he is one of those we are looking for. . . ."

"Perhaps you are right," another voice answered. "We must test him further. Perhaps he will survive. . . ."

IX

"Terry!"

He snapped awake at the sound of his name.

"Hey! Come on! Work to do!"

For a moment Terry sank back groggily, considering telling Tinkan to go to hell. But that was only for a moment. As he jumped from bed and began dressing, Grontunk's voice joined Tinkan's.

"Come on! How's a student supposed to learn anything around here? We've got three power stations to key back in."

Terry grinned. Grontunk's tone reminded him of all the Serious Sophomores at Berkeley, Notebooks at the Ready.

And he remembered Cal, teasing him his second year about his own voluminous note-taking. "*Listen with your mind, not that notebook,*" Cal had said then. And when he'd argued that he needed to refresh his memory with the notes, Cal had laughed at him, but he'd taught him the trick. "*You want to know exactly what was said in a classroom? Go back and be there and listen. Just picture the classroom around—get the details and the movement in the picture, and the little sounds real clear, and you'll find yourself listening to the professor again.*"

Finished dressing, Terry joined his companions in the corridor, and they headed for the cafeteria, over Grontunk's protests. "You mean you're going to feed your face when we've got work to do?" the Saurian complained.

"And how long have *you* been up?" Terry asked.

"We Saurians believe in working first, then eating. Seems more natural that way. But as a student . . ."

"But as a student," Terry answered, "best you take into account the eccentricities of your instructor."

"Who's being eccentric?" The gay voice from the dining hall was matched by the slim cool figure of Murtag.

"Good m.-morning," he stammered.

"You overslept," she said. "But I've already got a breakfast set out for you, and I gather we're not in too much of a rush, so I told the boys to let you sleep a few minutes anyhow."

"I find it a shame that we can't offer our friend Tinkan something," Grontunk growled. "He seems not to understand the partaking of food—though I suppose we could offer him a jolt of electricity or a bottle of oil, but that doesn't seem quite the same thing."

Murtag grinned. "I've never heard of a robot eating eggs for breakfast."

"I," said Tinkan somewhat solemnly, "have already reconciled myself to your animal habits. But I find a smooth-flowing intake of power to be much more efficient and . . ."

"*Eggs?*" Grontunk broke in. "You're eating *eggs?*"

"Whoa, boy. Simmer down," Terry said. "They're *not* Saurian eggs."

"Oh. Of course. But . . . oh, never mind. I see. It's

67

just another interspecies difference." Grontunk struggled with his own concept of anyone who would eat an egg, no matter who or whose.

"And what would you like?" Terry asked.

"Oh, a chunk of boiled *alup*." The word was foreign to Terry so he flipped on the translator. It replied in Galactic, "*Alup*: the young of a species of biped that . . ."

"*What?*" Murtag's reaction was as horrified as Grontunk's had been.

"All right, everybody simmer down." Terry waved at both of them. "So on a Saurian world such as Grontunk's, bipeds are good for breakfast; while on our worlds eggs are good. I think as long as we accept that neither his bipeds nor our eggs are the same as the ones that we're accustomed to at home, and that what we're actually getting is synthesized out of the computer's dispensary system anyhow, we can all forget the subject."

Terry changed the subject. "You say we've got some power stations to key back in?"

"Yes. The computer notified us an hour or more ago."

"Best we get on with the job then."

Finishing breakfast hastily, Terry led the way and they all descended to the grid control room. There routine took over, and three of them functioned smoothly as a team, while Grontunk took up a post as student observer just inside the control room door. The check was thorough, and eventually the power stations were brought into operation, phased in to match the grid, and switched into the combine.

At last Terry turned from the board. "Secure panels. End of routine. Work crew dismissed," and the formality dropped away from them as they headed back toward the cafeteria.

He was just beginning to say something when the floor swayed and fell from beneath them. Terry grabbed ineffectually for the wall, noting as he was falling that it was an entire section of flooring that had given way. There was a splash, and he found himself submerged in icy water. Cold and darkness made up the universe around him now, and Terry began to struggle. Strip out of clothes, automatic response told him; and desperately he kicked and shrugged.

68

The shirt came off and floated away in the darkness, and finally the clinging slacks and sandals followed, and he started swimming for the surface.

The orientation, he realized, had not taken over—but it was there, and within it was data he had to have. Even as he struggled for the surface, Terry summoned that portion of information dealing with being underwater. He was swimming wrong. Without hesitation he corrected the method, reaching the surface at last as he made the correction.

But it was not a surface of air. The water was flush with cold, hard stone.

His lungs were screaming for air, yet Terry knew he had the information on how to do without it; the knowledge was there, but he was almost scared to use it. He must have air, his lungs insisted. But the orientation package was assuring him that he could survive without air.

As though grasping at a last straw, Terry let the orientation take over. The pressure in the lungs slackened. Temporarily, the muscles slackened as well. The heartbeat that had been with him since birth came to a stop.

Terry felt detached, superconscious but not really aware of the body's functions. Then the muscles tautened again; the heart began to pump, but to a different rhythm; and there was no demand on his lungs. Chemical resources within the body that he had never been aware of before were operating, supplying in quick bursts the energy to drive the muscles, without oxygen.

Terry stirred and swam again. But still he was in the pitch black dark. Belatedly, he realized that in stripping out of his clothes he had also lost the cat-eyes, and the situation here was desperate. Without lights . . . the orientation answered him. Without light he must use another means of navigation—sound.

Terry put it into practice instantly, concentrating on the messages of his ears. But no, ears were designed for operation in air. Abruptly the sensory information came flowing to his brain—from his skin. As he relaxed, Terry was aware of other nearby motions. Surprisingly, he could identify them. Gronunk, off that way; Murtag. And Tinkan. But there was more information: the shell above him was hard,

69

solid. The chamber was not large. And there—toward Piet Murtag, an air surface over the water, and she was already swimming toward it.

Hurriedly now, with the new swimming motions he was becoming accustomed to, Terry swam after her. The surface was right ahead, and she broke it first, Terry close behind her. Almost simultaneously, the robot and then the Saurian broke through the water.

Terry was about to speak, when blackness engulfed him. His heart paused; his muscles slackened; and then there was a fierce demand. His mouth opened and a gush of stale air came out, expelled forcefully. He gasped and found himself breathing great lungsful of air. The anaerobic function was no longer required, and his lungs demanded that he catch up quickly, resupply the stored energies. For several moments his whole life seemed to hang on nothing but breathing while he floated lazily and relaxed, outstretched on the surface of the water.

Again he was about to speak when Piet dived and with his new sense of underwater "hearing," Terry could tell that she was moving away, back under the solid ledge, back in the direction from which they had come.

Gasping in a huge breath, Terry dived and followed, and was aware of the others following also. Then he realized why. The specifications of the building were plain before him. The exit from this subcellar was over here, and down. Terry began diving, feeling the wall as he approached, and the small doorway.

Open, his senses told him, and Piet had already passed through. Terry followed and was immediately aware of an open surface above him, but even as he rose he made his way toward the stairwell that he knew left from the room. The stairs were there, the water lapping gently at their top.

Terry crawled out and heard the others emerging behind him as he made his way up the last few steps. In the lighted corridor above, Piet was nowhere to be seen, but there were wet footprints leading away down the corridor. Terry was about to follow when he realized his own stark nakedness. Nope. Best he return to quarters now. Piet was ob-

70

viously okay, but she might not approve of being following at the moment.

Then he remembered his equipment—his five prize possessions—all lost with his clothing. Turning, Terry made his way back down the stairs, passing the robot and the Saurian, and dived back into the water. Surprising how well oriented he felt, now that he knew the way out.

Traveling with his new technique of underwater orientation, Terry made his way back to the original chamber, located his gear in total darkness, and began towing it out of the trap. Then he hesitated. Water in this room was wrong. His knowledge of the building indicated that it was an unused room, and that there was a water main . . .

Diving back down, trailing clothes and equipment in one hand, Terry located the water main and with his new-found navigational sense tried to get a picture of the break, and the extent of the damage. There was none. Instead, there was a valve where no valve was recorded in the details of his knowledges.

Experimentally, he opened it, and felt-heard a scream of high-pressure water coming from the pipe. Hastily he closed it again and turning, made his way back towards the stairs.

The valve had not been leaking. As far as he knew it didn't even belong there. And the floor that had caved in beneath them? It had reseated itself solidly in place the minute they were clear of it.

Emerging on the stairwell, Terry began to laugh. Somebody was playing games, but it hadn't been serious, it had been a good swim.

At the back of his mind Terry could see a repair robot installing that valve in a place where it didn't belong; while other robots carefully cut loose and hinged a section of flooring in the hall that the four free beings must pass. . . .

For some reason, he concluded, the computer had elected to give them all a swimming lesson.

Even as he questioned why, his memory located and his recall gave him in detail the answer. It was Piet's voice saying, ". . . *Of course the training program included orientation, but without using the orientation to the point where*

71

you had gone beyond what you had been given . . . well, it just wouldn't work."

As he emerged into the hall, Terry became conscious of the humming speaker system. Of course. The computer would have had to supervise the experiment. He spoke without looking around.

"Okay, Computer, are you listening?"

"Yes, Citizen Terry."

"My deduction is that you have decided to put us through a training program. Am I right?"

"Yes, Citizen Terry."

"May I inquire the extent of and reason for this program?"

This time there was a slight pause. Then, "The extent will be the limit you set yourself. The reason—your survival. And mine."

X

DAYS FLOWED into weeks and the weeks mounted in number, but the passage of time was scarcely observed. Their days were taken up with work and training, and an occasional nasty surprise cooked up by the computer to test survival reflexes. But the tasks were self-imposed and the computer kept pace with their progress.

The group was becoming well-knit and coordinated and no longer felt the necessity for filling the empty hall of the cafeteria with the loud sounds of bravado they had first employed to convince themselves they were not alone. Indeed, it would have seemed strange to them now for anyone at all to appear.

Terry found his flashes of anger becoming more violent as the pressures increased and no matter how he reminded himself that they were unreasonable, they recurred. Yet he couldn't show them. More and more he was falling into the category of accepted leader in their reach toward each goal; and from such a position he couldn't allow himself the weaknesses that might be acceptable in the others.

72

Even Tinkan was occasionally illogically annoyed as some of the more obvious points of a lesson were driven home by a barrage of repetition designed to refine mastery of a given point.

"If you've done a thing once," Tinkan was saying, "that should be sufficient."

"That," Terry insisted, his own annoyance vanishing, "is precisely the point. Without the experience of having made a connection with a particular set of facts we could be caught flat-footed in an emergency."

"But what emergency, Terry?" Murtag broke in with an intensity that startled them. "We've been at this for nearly a standard month, and I see no threat to my survival; I want to go home."

A standard Galactic month, Terry thought. It didn't sound long when you said it that way, but it worked out to nearly one and a quarter Earth years. Like the emergency itself, whatever it might be. Three hundred and seventy-three galactic years ago. Terry pictured the span of time in terms of Earth history. Approximately 5,520 years ago. Greece had appeared as a tiny settlement made by wandering tribes of Hellenes from the northwest, had grown her great culture, had disintegrated during a few months of those 373 galactic years. Rome had risen and fallen—but Rome was a comparatively recent event in this chronology.

Five thousand five hundred years ago. What would have been happening on Earth? That would have been just after the building of the Great Pyramid of Cheops; the time of King Solomon's mines. That would have been about the time of the Minotaur—just before the destruction of the flourishing civilization of Crete, the mysterious fire-and-earthquake sequences that had destroyed first Cnossus and then each of the Cretan cities in turn.

What had Murtag been saying? That she didn't see a threat to her survival—didn't see a threat in a catastrophe so great that an outpost planet had been forgotten since almost before the beginning of Earth's history?

He turned to the girl fiercely. "The fact that you see no threat to your survival is, in itself, a threat to your survival," he stated flatly.

73

"What? I don't follow you."

"The fact that you see no threat and can't imagine one. The fact that you spent your entire life in safety and security, wrapped up in a nice cozy little civilization that protected you even though you knew next to nothing of the technical details of its operation. Do you realize that your disaster was almost simultaneous with a nearly prehistoric time on my own planet when flourishing civilizations suddenly disappeared—but that on my own world we have grown and grown again civilizations that put those first ones to shame? Yet you're so wrapped up in your wrecked one that you can't understand that something must have happened to it or we wouldn't be trapped here. Use your head, Murtag. When the computer said that there was a threat to our survival, it didn't mean something that it knew all about and we didn't. It meant something unknown. And it didn't mean that we were going to have to meet it immediately; it meant that we were going to have to prepare for it. You seem to have the idea," he continued brutally, "that this is all some sort of a silly game, and shortly you can go back to being Pietra, safe and secure in your civilization's arms. For all your knowledge, you seem to have very little conception of the size of this universe, and the threats that exist in it."

The harsh savagery met no resistance in the girl. Instead Terry was amazed to see her face whiten, and she answered in a small, scared voice.

"I know," she said. "Something terrible must have happened. But . . ."

"But it is up to us to find out what," Terry stated fiercely. "And it's up to us to be prepared to meet any possibility we can train ourselves to meet. We can't stay here forever. But we would be darned fools to go out against an unknown without being as prepared as we can get."

"I feel very well prepared," Grontunk interjected. "In fact, if I went home now, I would be greatly respected. My fame as a wise man would ring through the ages of Saurian history. There are no threats on my home planet that I could not meet."

"Mmmm. Perhaps. On my planet people too far in ad-

74

vance of their civilization haven't normally met with honor. Quite the reverse." He smiled grimly.

"How would you feel about yourself if you went back now, knowing that your world is an outpost of a Galactic Civilization, probably to be swallowed up by that civilization on its next wave of expansion—and yet didn't know what insanities existed in that civilization to let us be trapped here? You couldn't warn your world what to expect, when you only knew that a tremendously huge Galactic Civilization exists, but not what the factors are.

"How could you," he asked fiercely, "go back without going forward first?"

And he couldn't do it. He couldn't go back until he had gone forward. He longed for the green hills of Earth so deeply it was an aching pain; he admitted within himself that he wanted to go home—as badly as Murtag did.

The difference was that he knew he couldn't; and he knew, too, that the barrier that prevented him, or would prevent him when the opportunity came, was nothing imposed from without, but a hard-held recognition of responsibility from within; and that not sloughing that responsibility would be a far greater task than any other he had set himself.

"No," he said, softly this time, "we can't any of us go back, not until we find out the nature of the problem that exists beyond the . . . door . . . to this tiny world."

Then, shifting the subject quickly, he turned to Tinkan. "It seems to me that this transposer theory we're working on might make a convenient method for giving you that independent power supply. And perhaps us, as well. I'd not mind," he mused, "having something like a one hundred kilowatt generator that I could slip in my hip pocket, just for emergency uses, say, on backward worlds or something."

"No I guess you wouldn't," Tinkan answered, "but you know it's never been done, don't you? The very smallest transposers take more equipment than you could pack on your back."

Grontunk interrupted. "Terry, how could you hope to build such a device here?"

Terry looked around at the room they'd fitted up as a combination study room and lab, and at the equipment that

75

took up most of its area. "Why not? Oh, I see. You mean the computer might worry about it? But—we've got a shielded room here, and surely a few controlled experiments wouldn't be out of order." He grinned suddenly. "You suppose we could get permission to try?"

He walked over to the wall and keyed an intercom. "Computer," he said, releasing the button as the loudspeaker system hum answered him, "I'd like permission to try . . . to try . . ." Suddenly he was very self-conscious. It hadn't been done before, Tinkan had said, in all the great Galactic civilization.

"Permission to try what?" The computer's tones, as blandly mechanical as ever, brought him out of the negation.

"Permission to try building a small transposer device for experimental purposes. One, say, with a range of five feet inside this shielded room. I think I can make a pocket-size power pack, using the basics behind the big transposer. Would that be out of order?"

There was a definite pause, and the computer hummed a bit before answering. "I have no record of such a small transposer. Have you data that leads to the conclusion that you might be able to build such?"

"Yes. It's a matter of using the theory in a different context, but the basics are actually the same. I think it'll work."

"Very well. Permission to try. Except—you will use the wrecked power station, Number P-12, on the far side of the planet, thus endangering as little of the station as possible, and only yourself in case you fail."

It was a reasonable precaution, Terry realized, nodding to himself. "Okay. But how do I get there? Walk?"

"Transportation will be afforded you. But you should specify in advance what equipment you will need, including how long you'll be there and any other details necessary to the stocking and environmental control factors of the place."

Rapidly, Terry reeled off a list of the tools and components he'd need and ended with a request for the services of a repair-robot, when Tinkan interrupted.

"I have a great interest in this," Tinkan said. "I should like to be your assistant."

76

"How about it, Computer?"

"Yes." The computer did not amplify its permission. "I . . . uh . . . should like to witness from a distance," Grontunk stated diffidently.

"Can you add a video circuit so the others may watch from here?" Terry asked.

"It will be added."

"Terry? I . . . will you be very careful, please?" Murtag's voice sounded small in the large room.

"Sure," Terry grinned.

"He will indeed." The voice of the computer came through the speaker grill with some force. "And I have added several things to his list to make certain that he is. For example, the station is solidly built with a number of special safeguards."

"I shall want to know if there is a method of safeguarding the far terminal of this device until I have ranged it in," Terry inquired.

"The young student is suddenly cautious," Tinkan said mockingly. "There's an obvious answer to that question, Terry. The transposer is always associated with a computer for just that reason. In the event of mixed-up coordinates, the computer can act instantly to turn off the transposition before violent damage results. I suspect until you prove the range of your unit to be very precise indeed, such a control will have to be maintained over it."

"Correct," the computer answered. "The original discovery of the transposer device has not yet been made known to you, but suffice it to say that the originator of the concept failed to outlive the first experiment."

"I see. But he left records and others took over?" Terry asked.

"No," the computer answered. "He left only one record—a cavity in his home world, nearly a mile in diameter. Very little work has been done on it since," the computer continued, "and the theory is no better today than it was at the end of the first investigation. You will, of course, report to the orientation room for a full orientation on this subject before leaving for the experimental site."

"I thought I already had one," Terry muttered.

"You should know better," Murtag said. "You're not

given a full orientation on any subject until you at least show you know what it's about."

"Okay." Terry shrugged. "Let's get on with it."

Three days later Terry was informed that the old power station had been converted into a site from which he might start work. At the last minute, he began wondering what the planet outside would look like on the trip around it, but as he and Tinkan approached the departure room, he recognized that he was not about to find out. The trip would be by transposer, of course.

Shrugging off his disappointment, Terry stepped into the transposer room, felt the disquieting effect that had brought him here over an Earth year ago, and suddenly found himself standing in the corner of a large room that was part of a power plant.

Here, none of the refinements in the box-like room left behind him had been maintained. Terry glanced curiously at the exposed parts of the transposer grid above and around him. A hasty job indeed, was his first conclusion; but then he realized that the transposer unit itself must have been here all along, intended for use only for robots and supplies, and the unit had never been beautified, concealed and protected as it would have been if intended for citizen use.

Nor had the rest of the power station. Parts that would not be hurt by exposure were exposed; those requiring housing for mechanical efficiency were housed, strictly on a basis of practicality.

Terry's gaze wandered here and there about the room, seeking points of knowledge and understanding in the confusion, but it was as though he were at home in a familiar workshop. Each item seemed to supply its own history to his gaze, and each interlocking machine the interlocking concepts that caused its presence here.

Terry recognized a large pile of those items he had ordered for his experiment. Tinkan was already moving toward the pile with the air of a person so preoccupied with getting something done that he had no time for idle chatter. Terry pitched in and the two began sorting and moving the materials to the room where they would set up the experiment.

Hours later Murtag's voice came through to them with the ethereal non-directness of a speaker system.

"You characters going to work all night?"

With a start, Terry realized that he had given no consideration to rest or comfort, allowing his intentness and preoccupation to drive him almost beyond endurance.

"Right. Time to knock off for a while."

He stretched luxuriously, and turned to Tinkan, still busy at the bench they had set up.

"Time to go," he said.

"Sure, Terry. Go ahead."

Terry looked fondly at the robot, bent over his tasks. The robot could keep on after his own—he smiled wryly, thinking of Tinkan's expression—"biochemical makeup" demanded rest. Turning away from his work, Terry activated the transposer and arrived at the base room.

And so it went. Day after day he and Tinkan worked, each at his own pace, and time after time Terry was called from his labors by Murtag's faintly reproving voice. And occasionally Tinkan left, too, for his own periods of "retreat for compution."

At last the lab equipment was set up, the components fitted, the experiment ready. The experimental device itself was, as Terry had predicted, very small indeed, quite capable of being combined into a light-weight packet; but there were literally tons of instruments surrounding it to detect its every action, to check each erg of energy; and fail-safe devices that could operate on a nearly-instantaneous basis.

It was time for testing and all was in readiness. Terry and Tinkan were seated at the control boards in the far room, finishing the final check.

"Tinkan," he said, almost softly as though afraid of being overheard, though the intercom system was only switched on when needed, "shall we do a preliminary test just for ourselves? I mean," he added, sensing a quick negative from the robot, "Murtag and Grontunk have been worrying up a storm. She . . . she's not really used to taking many chances, you know."

79

"Sure, Murtag's worried, but she's been very careful not to interfere or impose her worries on us. And—would it be fair to rule them out?" Tinkan reasoned.

"Hell, I guess you're right at that. Okay," he said, "we key them in as well as the computer." He flipped the intercom and video switch.

"Ready to test," he said formally.

"You've finished final checks?" the computer asked.

"Yes, all set," Terry answered. "Is our audience over there awake?"

"Right here, Terry," came Murtag's voice, a little shrill; and Grontunk's voice followed: "We're watching."

"Good enough," Terry said. "Okay. Permission to proceed?"

"We have a good set of notes and recordings on your activities," the computer informed him. "Proceed with the experiment."

Terry's attention, then, went to the board, and to the small video that showed him the tiny instrument in the room beyond, backed by its massive array of control and recording equipment. He pushed the activating button.

At first nothing happened, but that was to be expected. Unlike the larger machines, this one depended on a momentary time-lapse in which to warm up.

Then a needle flicked; and another. And there was a sudden roar as though a mighty wind surged through the building and Terry as well.

There was a stretching sensation, and Terry realized it was his hand, reaching for the cut-off switch. But the roar of the wind and the feel of his out-stretched hand persisted, going on and on, as the unreal-looking board seemed to dissolve before him.

XI

THE IMPRESSION that "things" had disappeared lasted for seconds—or an infinity of time, Terry wasn't sure which. Then, gradually, the control board coalesced before him. His hand was still poised before it, but he himself felt numb and vacuous as though somehow only half real. He was breathing but with a slow inertia of reaction that barely moved his chest, that seemed as tenuous as the control board or the room.

With concentrated effort, Terry moved his unreal hand toward the unreal control board. With more concentrated effort he made decimal decisions as to what to do, each seeming to take an infinity of time.

Not the cut-off switch. The hand wavered, still following its former instructions, then swung across the unreal panel and descended on another button.

Abruptly there was pressure and reality around him again; with a *cru-ump*, as though he had fallen a thousand miles, Terry was back in his seat, and time was moving again in a normal sequence.

Quickly Terry's hand reached now for the cut-off button, and even as he touched it, he began receiving communications from those who were watching.

"It's open again. They're alive!" Grontunk's voice.

"Terry! Are you all right?" This from Murtag.

And from the computer: "Please give a brief report as quickly as possible so that we may judge any necessary attentions you may need."

"I seem to be clear-headed, and all in one piece," Terry reported slowly. "Tinkan?"

"Solid again, and I seem to be functioning properly," he said briefly.

Terry grinned. "No emergency help needed at this time." He was checking the various panels for information even as he spoke, and then he turned to the video screen that showed the tiny transposer sitting serenely on its bench, apparently unharmed—an enigma that was offering no answers.

Quite apparently it operated. But what had it done? Something quite outside of that which had been predicted from what little was known of transposer theory, of that he was certain.

Terry directed a question to the big computer. "You were observing from several points outside the station. What were the reports?"

"Points one through five lost contact completely. The cam-

81

era at point six, approximately twelve stads from the power station, continued to function but showed a large globe that was not penetrated by its vision."

"Reproduction, please," Terry ordered, and on a separate video plate to the side there appeared a large, luminous ball and one part of his mind shrieked "Atomic explosion!" but the ball neither receded nor expanded; it was simply there, a gold fringed blackness.

"Is this a still or an action shot?"

"It is a still, but there was no action. The ball lasted as shown for the 33 minutes, 25.5 seconds that the experiment continued, and then simply disappeared. showing"—the picture changed—"the station as it normally appears."

Terry glanced at the chronometer on his wrist. "I have here . . ." Terry read the figures off. "Will you check that with the exact time now?"

"Your chronometer seems to have lost 33 minutes, 15.5 seconds."

"And that," Terry said, "checks beautifully with my impression that I was only in there for a few seconds. Compute the time rate differential between my chronometer and your records . . . oh, never mind. I've got it myself. It's about 2,000 to one. This thing might make a dilly of a time capsule of some sort."

"Yes." Tinkan spoke up from his board wryly. "I think we've just rediscovered the 'cooler' principle, though this is the first time I've ever heard of anybody getting from inside out under his own steam."

Terry felt a little let down, then brushed the feeling aside. "I thought I had a complete course on this subject?"

"On transposition, not on its tangential usages," the computer answered.

"Okay. Let's get on with it. Did other observation points report anything else?"

"The same phenomenon was recorded on all the more distant cameras." As Terry watched, the scene shifted but remained the same. From a further distance it could be seen that the globe was indeed spherical and apparently haloed,

82

but otherwise impenetrable, so far as the camera's eyes were concerned.

"Very well, that's the way it looked with light. How about some of the other sensors?"

"The same stations that reported blank on optical reported blank on every other sense impression. Those that continued to function reported a blankness or impenetrability of the size and shape seen by the video equipment. Heat was neither emitted nor absorbed. Radar showed a perfect reflecting surface, with nothing beyond. No energy was recorded as either entering or leaving the sphere."

"I see." Terry sat back and relaxed, and then began firing a series of questions couched in mathematical terms which the computer could answer far more quickly than he could calculate.

"How does this compare with your system of 'cooling' beings?" Terry, having found out all he could about his own experiment, went back to the "tangential" effect he had just experienced.

"Not closely." The computer paused and then went on. "Since you have noticed the connection, I will of course give you a briefing on that subject at the next opportunity. But in general, the difference is that when it becomes necessary to 'cool' a being, as you express it, the being is stunned and placed in a recyclic transposer field which has no other terminal. The energy to sustain the continuing transpositions is recycled and therefore not considered to be a particularly large power drain. Such recycling can go on indefinitely but so far as I know no experiments have ever been made that determined a time differential between the inside and the outside of the field. We simply knew that so long as a being was kept in the field, he did not appreciably deteriorate. The system has also been used in the storage and preservation of perishable food products."

"I see." Terry was amused at his own horrified reaction when the computer so casually juxtaposed the two usages of the effect. "What is the longest period that beings have been maintained in a cooling system?" he asked.

"Never in any event more than one Galactic . . ." Abruptly the voice cut off and the speaker carried an extra hum as though the computer had lost its thread of reasoning—or something had overridden the response. Then it resumed: "That is a security matter than I cannot reveal at this time."

Terry stared at the video panel before him, alarm bells ringing in his mind. This was the first time as a student he had run into any indication that technical knowledge would or could be withheld except on the basis of ability to grasp that knowledge.

Aloud he said, "Very well. Prepare for the next experiment."

"Terry! No!" It was Pietra's voice, followed by immediate contrition. "I beg your pardon. Do . . . do, of course, as you think best." The voice was tight with self-control.

"Come on back and let's talk over your results first," Grontunk's voice came over the speaker.

"Sorry, no," Terry answered briefly, and then as though in afterthought, "Tinkan, what do you report?"

"Not a thing, Terry. There seems to be a total blank spot. I saw you touch the initiation button, and I saw your meters begin to read, and then nothing. I'm sure it was something"—the robot continued sounding puzzled—"but it was nothing. I . . . well, it seems silly, but I felt—stretched."

"Yeah," Terry muttered. Then: "That was the time factor! Of course. There are some adjustments we'd better make that we can't make from here. Next experiment postponed for physical adjustment," he said officially, and stood up from the board. "Come on, Tinkan."

The manual adjustments in the next room didn't take long, and within thirty minutes Terry and Tinkan were back at their boards. Speakers and video still hummed on, and Terry said firmly, "Permission to conduct second test."

"Permission granted," the computer said, and Terry was grateful that neither Murtag nor Grontunk said anything.

Again he reached out and touched the initiation button. Again there was a pause before the needles flicked and swung smoothly up to show a steady operation.

Terry's gaze riveted on the video screen to the next room. The enigma sat there, quietly glowing, except—there. A tiny ball of blackness, scarcely visible, was inside the miniature transmission cage—and another, six feet away, was hanging over the bench in empty space.

Carefully, Terry scanned the instruments. Then, "Permission to inspect the device in operation," he said.

"Is video not sufficient?"

"Well, I can see the thing's operating, but the fields are so small I can hardly see them through video."

"Why don't you move the camera up closer, Terry?" This logical question from Tinkan.

"Oh." He felt a moment of frustration. He had completely forgotten he had remote control over the lab camera.

Operating the focusing controls, he brought the picture closer and closer until the transposer cage filled the screen, and the tiny black dot within it swelled with the rest of the picture. It was just that—an impenetrable black dot.

Swinging the camera, Terry found the other dot. The two were identical, size for size, totally black, and that was that.

Bringing another remote control instrument into operation, Terry backed the camera off until he had both dots in the field of vision. Then he swung a manipulator arm over, picked up a piece of plastic tubing from the bench, and poked at the dot outside the cage with that. The plastic bent, but the dot stayed where it was.

Picking up a small chunk of wire with the manipulator, Terry poked again. The wire bent away and the dot remained where it was.

The manipulator moved again, picked up a hammer, and swung it forcefully at the dot. The hammer stopped as though striking a brick wall, and there was a distinct *clang* through the audio circuits. Terry drew the hammer back and brought it before the eye of the video camera. There, in the hard steel face was a round indentation, precisely conforming to the figure of the dot.

Terry sat for several seconds gazing at the various dials and back at the video image. Then he reached out and moved one of the dials cautiously.

The dot expanded. Terry moved another dial. The dot, hanging free over the bench, moved. Terry swung the dial further, and the dot seemed to jump. He turned it back the other way and the dot jumped back.

85

Bringing the manipulator back into play, Terry selected a large brick and set it on the table directly in the path of the dot's motion, then moved the dot again. It edged up to the brick and pushed. The brick moved.

Terry wiggled the dial again and watched the brick skitter across the table. Then he moved it back and, with the manipulator also, moved the brick back. This time he left the manipulator holding the brick and reached out, flicking the dial quickly.

The black dot seemed to have disappeared and reappeared on the other side of the brick, and when Terry brought the brick toward the face of the camera there was a small neat hole punched right through it.

"Did you get all that?" Terry asked.

"Yes."

"The equations . . ." Terry rambled off a half dozen mathematical terms, then finished, "Okay. End of second experiment," as he carefully phased the dot out of existence and turned off the panel.

"Very interesting, Terry," Tinkan admitted, "but that's like no transposer field I ever saw."

"Right, and at the same time wrong. You are quite correct it is like no transposer field you ever saw, but when before have you ever seen a transposer field from the outside? The transposer in use produces a very brief flash of the same sort of field we have here, but remember: first, the transposer field as used is designed to get something from one place to another; and second, it uses an external power supply. It takes megawatts of energy to keep the field going, and that's why they don't keep it going. In this case"—Terry waved at the video picture— "the energies are designed to be reentrant so the field can maintain itself once set up.

"That doesn't make it any more useful as a transposer, but it definitely can give it some other functions. The differential time factor involved in existence inside the field shows in effect that what we have is not one but a pair of closed universes. Sort of like taking a zero and converting it into plus and minus one. Of course our conversion equations don't necessarily have to come out to plus and minus one, they can come out to plus and minus any number you could care to name.

"That same time effect that caused you to feel 'stretched' always occurs inside the transpower field, but since it has always been operated so briefly it had never become apparent as anything more than a slight jump in reality to people using the field. Let's go ahead and set up experiment three," he continued. "I'm right anxious to find out what our tcy can do now."

As they started into the laboratory, Tinkan said, "I think I follow what you're saying about this gadget, but perhaps I haven't come to the same conclusions. You said you thought it could make a power supply for me. Do you still think so?"

"That's what we're about to find out. I can see two ways of doing it, just off hand. One, we can use the matter-transposing feature to shift an electrical current through space from anywhere that it's available to the receiver. Since there are plenty of places in space where you can tap a steady electrical flow due to the energy potentials say, near a star, it would seem that this might be a good route to follow.

"The other method would be to use the spatial separation between the two fields to, perhaps, drive a small mechanical device." Terry reached out and picked up the brick, examining it closely. "This hole indicates that we have quite a lot of energy that could be used that way."

"But, Terry, didn't that come from the energy you applied in shifting the field?"

"In a manner of speaking, yes. But . . ." Terry paused. "No. You're right. I guess I hadn't thought that one all the way through yet." He went over and examined one of the recorders sitting on another bench, then spoke an equation to the computer and got an answer. "Right. The energy required to penetrate the brick came from the control circuits, so I guess we don't have perpetual motion after all. At least, not quite that way." He turned back to the bench. "I guess we're ready to start modifying baby, now."

With the two of them working, the little device on the bench rapidly changed shape. The tiny transposing cage

87

became a dual cage, with a pair of heavy power leads running from it connecting to some sensing instruments and a resistor that Terry had salvaged from some of the old power generating equipment in the station. By the time they were through the little enigma had been so changed as to be hardly recognizable; was, in fact, almost two units coupled together.

Terry seated himself at the panel. "Permission to start test three," he said.

"Go ahead."

"Coordinates of maximum concentration for the plus and minus charges trapped in the planet's magnetic field," Terry ordered, and as the computer answered he began shifting dials.

Just as he was reaching for the red button that would initiate action, the board went blank and the computer said, "Test suspended."

Terry looked up in surprise. "Why?" he asked.

"The coordinates you asked for. My data indicates that the relative charge between these points would be of an order of magnitude that you could not possibly handle with the equipment you've got. Since I am in charge of the safety of this planet, I think I need some more information before you . . ."

"Oh. You worry too much. The proposed experiment," Terry began outlining, "is to remove charged particles from one cubic centimeter of the general area of densest negative charge in one of the radiation belts, and to cancel it against an equal quantity of positive charge in the other belt. The actual quantity of charge transferred will be proportional to the number of transpositions per second, and since there will be no direct connection during the transposition period . . ."

The board lit up again. "Go ahead," the computer said.

Terry reached out and touched the initiation switch, and watched the dials closely as the little test transposer began to warm up. Then he focused the camera close in toward the cages and observed the two tiny black dots standing within.

"So far so good," he muttered, and reached for another

88

dial. The dots disappeared with tiny, bright flashes as the trapped charge particles within them dispersed, collected on the terminals, and flowed through the circuit.

Terry turned his inspection on the tiny pulses that had gone through the recording mechanism. Not very much current per pulse. He moved a dial and the little black dots reappeared, now surrounded by tiny halos which Terry recognized as the intermittent on-and-off action of the transposer spheres. He advanced the knob again. The faint crackle from the device turned to a tiny mosquito buzz, and a pale blue flame appeared above one of the cages. Terry inspected the readings again. A fair quantity of electric charge was now flowing through the external test circuit as the number of transpositions increased.

"That flame," he pointed out to Tinkan, "is caused by the protons we're drawing in. Once they're canceled by the electrons in the other cage they're simply hydrogen atoms, but hot enough to catch fire and burn spontaneously in air." He moved one of the dials and the flame disappeared. "Now we have our cake and can eat it too, or something to that effect," he said. "The transposer field can work both ways on that side and if we make the outgoing field only slightly bigger than the incoming field, it will act to trap all the hydrogen and kick it back where it came from. That would be a little bit better than carrying a candle around on our backs, perhaps?"

"Perhaps," said Tinkan. "A bit."

Now Terry turned the knob that controlled the transposition frequency again, and the mosquito buzz turned into a whine; needles began ticking over to higher and yet higher readings. He reached out and inched the knob, and this time was rewarded with a loud *"spla-att."* All the dials dropped back to zero, while in the video picture before him the test circuit attached to the two cages was a smoking ruin, the huge power resistor still glowing on its supports, at a white heat; and the cables had melted and run like water, leaving tiny droplets across the bench.

"Too bad, Terry," Grontunk's voice came over the loudspeaker. "Just as you got it going good."

But Terry grinned. "What do you mean, too bad? I

89

was drawing better than half a megawatt of power before it blew up! And under perfect control at that. Looks like we've got your power supply, Tinkan. Test completed."

Terry reached for the cut-off button and touched it even as Tinkan's voice was saying, "Hey, wait!"

Too late, Terry realized his goof as the laboratory shuddered and shook, and the screen before him went dark. There was a faint hiss, and Terry realized that air was escaping, or rushing in.

"Damn," he said. "I forgot to phase it out, and E still equals MC^2."

"Come on, Terry, let's get out of here before your biochemical system gets all fouled up with this bad atmosphere."

Hastily, the two retreated to the transposer and back to the main base. There they headed immediately for the classroom, as they called the local lab. "Hey, Computer," Terry shouted as he walked in, "let's have some pics of that last experiment."

Vaguely he noticed the others weren't there, but promptly on the screen appeared the picture of the old power station sitting calmly, in its desert location. And then serenity vanished. A whole wall of the huge structure seemed to come apart in the manner of a jigsaw puzzle, and behind it a bright light glared. Then the scene went dark as a hurtling object smashed toward and obviously into the camera.

"Wow!" Terry said. "That's bigger than I thought it was. And I'm glad there wasn't very much M in that MC^2. Have you got any of the energy readings from the instruments?"

Terry and the computer were busy for some time examining and discussing the details of the experiment, but eventually it was over and Terry headed out of the laboratory, a somewhat silent and bemused Tinkan following him.

"Your power supply may need a few bugs worked out," Tinkan observed. "I'm glad I wasn't wearing *that* in my circuitry."

"Details," Terry answered. "Minor details. Come on, let's go home."

"Home?"

"Yeah. That's were the food is. I figure," he added as they stepped into the corridor leading to the cafeteria, "that it won't take more than a couple of weeks now to outfit you with a good . . ." He stopped as he heard the sound of sobs in the distance. "Murtag?" he called.

"*TERRY!*" Murtag appeared, running down the corridor and flung herself at him. His arms opened of their own accord, and she was within them before either of them realized it. Then they each drew back self-consciously.

"You . . . you're safe, Terry. I saw that explosion. . . ." Murtag was blushing and her voice ran slowly down. Terry opened his mouth to stammer something in reply when Grontunk saved the situation by arriving, with a gruff, "Welcome back, Terry! Tinkan! Glad to see you both intact." And the big Saurian thumped them each on the back.

"The screen went blank in an explosion," Murtag began explaining, "and we didn't dare interrupt the computer to ask, because it might be busy saving your lives, and . . ."

"The screen went blank?" Then in a different tone, "Oh. I guess the video cable ran through the lab. Sorry. I hadn't realized you were cut off. But the experiments are over now, and, uh . . ."

"And he thinks I'm going to have one of those things wired into my innards." Tinkan's voice was reproachful. "Sometimes I wonder about the beings I pick for friends."

"Why, it ought to be safe enough, if you don't try to run a whole city with it. Anyhow," Terry declared firmly, "you're not the only one that's going to have one of those wired into your circuits. Of course, it's going to take some doing, to wire one into *my* circuits, but I think we can manage it. And you and Grontunk as well," he said to Murtag. "It looks to me like the best bet we've got—not only for getting around fast, when exploring, but also for bringing force to bear on any problem that we may run into. Among other things, if we set the flicker rate just right, and put the other terminal into a proper source of atmosphere, we could even explore worlds like this where the atmosphere doesn't quite meet our standards."

91

"What do you mean, wired in, Terry?" Grontunk sounded nervous.

"Just exactly what I said. In order to be fully effective, the field would have to be under your personal control by the most direct possible route. The most direct possible route that I can conceive of is a direct connection between the controls and the computer—that's your brain—that's controlling. In other words, a direct connection to a motor circuit that you can learn to control. I guess we'll have to do a bit of experimenting to find out just where the best areas of contact can be made; and of course the actual circuitry, the generator, if you wish to call it that, can be a backstrap—a pack or something of that sort, though I see no reason why we couldn't build that part in, too. The field effect isn't really dependent on the cage, and the rest of the circuitry can be extremely miniaturized. . . ."

"I begin to see several possibilities here," Tinkan interrupted. "The second field, as you showed, can be used to apply force through distance. And I gather that you can set the force point up wherever you desire to put it. This would mean"—he pointed to one of the automat units in the cafeteria they were just entering—"that I could actually reach inside one of those gadgets by materializing a point in it, and then move things around. I have seen times when this ability would have been very useful! Even if I couldn't see what I was doing. But wait—Terry! Could the field be worked as a video circuit? Could you actually see what the remote point was doing?"

"I hadn't thought of that, but I don't see why not. I think probably an extremely small point operating at a reasonably high flicker rate could be used to trap photons as well as particles, and we can certainly effect a shield so that trapped particles are replaced right back where they came from. It should give a rather good remote viewpoint. Sort of a keyhole in space. Actually," he continued, "it's already been done. That's how they set the transposer on various planets in the first place. But apparently nobody ever thought to apply it on a small scale."

"Or if they did," Pietra said, "perhaps they kept very

quiet about it. Can you imagine what a peepshow that would be? Used by an unethical populace?"

"Of course the other half of that equation," Grontunk said, "is the hole in the brick. Do you realize what a weapon that would be?"

Terry grinned. "That too. Okay, let's get back to the lab and start putting these devices together. We're going to have a lot of consequences to work out, and a lot of control circuits to figure, but . . ."

"But I begin to smell action." Grontunk snapped his jaws playfully, the huge set of Saurian teeth making a ferocious gnash.

That night as Terry lay in bed his mind took off in another direction.

They would be able to go now, to find out, to explore—but would they be ready? Each of them had grown in knowledge and responsibility, and it would be at least another twenty to thirty Galactic weeks more before the contraptions were ready for use.

But had they grown enough? he asked himself, and realized the incident that had set the worry in the forefront of his mind. Grontunk. Grontunk's *"But I begin to smell action. . . ."* and the gnashing of his huge, Saurian teeth.

Were he and his band of three going out against the whole galaxy as warriors, with a show of force that could only destroy them? Were they going as explorers—who might be stepped upon before their presence was even recognized? As technicians—in a civilization where technology had already been advanced for thousands of years? As supervisors to a race where those willing to assume the responsibility, he reminded himself, had dropped to a few entities per billion? That was the most logical answer, he thought—a lack of supervisors, and the concentration of their services in the galactic centers.

But—he didn't know. He only knew he didn't feel adequate to the task, whatever that task might turn out to be.

The voices didn't disturb him. Terry barely registered

them, though he vaguely remembered having heard them before.

"Our protégé advances rapidly. Already in some ways he has surpassed us."

"Will he then be one of the answers?"

"Ask, rather, whether we can afford his answers. He has found a way to wake the robots."

"Do you then consider destruction?"

"Not yet."

XII

TIME PASSED as model after model of the tiny transposers was built and tested; but not all of the time was spent on this task. Terry and Murtag had begun research into the bio-circuitry necessary to provide data links as direct as possible between motor nerves and external devices; while Grontunk and Tinkan were busy reasoning out as many functions as possible following on the basic concept.

Not all of the units that they developed would be directly attached to motor nerves, but all of them would be portable; for the range of possible applications proved great, running from the small power packs originally predicted, through video units, probes—a wide variety of functions.

There was one unit that pleased Grontunk especially—a hand weapon which would materialize one of the tiny spheres just outside of itself and then move it rapidly through space to a controlled distance. When tested, this one proved to be extremely accurate, admirably adjustable for range, and quite effective in making holes in things.

The point could be made so tiny and placed so accurately that it became a microscope capable of penetrating living tissue and observing what went on within it; a microscope that Terry was pleased to find was also quite capable of serving as a microknife, or a microprobe suitable for taking samples of living tissue or simply taking electrical readings between two points in the tissue. Eventually the points were found and plotted that could best be used for controlling the devices, and the taps were made—not with points or wire, but with the fields themselves.

The work took more time than Terry had estimated, and the thirty weeks he'd allotted became thirty-five, then forty, before he finally decided the time had come. They were in the cafeteria practicing at the time, and Terry was using his viewpoint to watch Tinkan's internal manipulation of one of the food units.

Terry moved his viewpoint off a couple of millimeters, as Tinkan's viewpoint went around making rapid taps on a series of relay points. The machine began to whir, and Terry withdrew, using his eyes to watch the results.

Out popped a complete meal, and Terry was about to rise and bring it back to the table, when it disappeared.

Murtag laughed and asked, "Where were you going?"

Terry looked down to see the food sitting before him. "Oh. Yeah. Well, we're getting pretty good control now," Terry said.

"Seems like it. I'm beginning to think of these gadgets and use 'em like an extra set of hands," Murtag said.

"I am very happy with my remote control sphere—say, what are we going to call these things? We can't say Remote Control Transpower sphere every time we want to refer to 'em, especially if we're in a hurry," Grontunk said.

"Maybe best you don't call them at all," Tinkan said mildly. "For all I know they might start answering back."

"That's one of the things I've been waiting for you guys to realize they could do. At least they make a pretty good audio pipe. Hadn't you noticed? You adjust the field this way. . . ." Terry demonstrated, his voice coming from a sphere at the other end of the hall as he continued speaking.

"Does it work the other way, too?"

"Sure it does." Murtag's voice came also from the other end of the hall. "Hi, Terry."

"Hi!" Terry grinned. Then he phased out his sphere and turned to the group at the table. "It seems to me that we've got these tools just about fitted up to the point where we can really use them. Any of you feel like going off and finding out what's wrong with the galaxy?"

95

"Sure, Terry," Grontunk answered promptly. "That's what I've been wanting to do all the time."

"I guess so." Murtag's voice seemed to hold a bit of doubt. "If you think we're ready. But . . . are we really ready?"

"No, but we never will be really ready, and I don't think we should wait much longer, now that we've got the means to go and a few tools to use."

"We have a problem," Tinkan interrupted. "Understandably we do not wish to go up against an unknown danger without being prepared for that danger. Equally understandably we cannot be prepared until we know what the danger is."

"And," Terry added, "we can't know what the danger is until we go find out. I say we go find out."

"Me, too," Grontunk said enthusiastically.

"Well, when you put it that way . . ." Murtag left the sentence hanging.

"Have you decided where we're going first, Friend Terry?" Tinkan asked.

"Yes. I've picked out five representative planets."

"When do we leave?" Grontunk's voice held a thrilled growl of excitement.

"How about that, Computer? When can we prepare an expedition to leave for Pranje?"

"The government center, Terry?" Murtag asked. "No one ever goes there. That is, unless they're officially invited."

"I plan," said Terry, "for us to write our own invitation."

"Permission denied," the computer's voice came flatly over the speaker system.

"Oh? Why?" Terry's voice held a smooth mildness that startled the other three.

"I cannot permit you to leave until I have open communications channels through which you can leave. I have no such open channels."

Terry was about to interrupt but the computer continued. "I cannot permit you to go into unknown territory until I can ascertain that you will be safe there."

"And how do you propose," Terry asked, "to get the information leading to such assurances?"

"We must wait for instructions." The computer's voice was

its usual monotone. Only the words were uncompromising. "You have a shortage of Supervisors. You should use every effort to find out why."

"On the contrary. I have at present no shortage of Supervisors, and my basic conditioning requires that I keep the former shortage from recurring."

"Oh? You mean we can't leave?"

"I do not consider it within the best interests. . . ." The voice dribbled off.

"Okay," said Terry. "Let's go."

"But Terry. We can't. The computer won't let us."

"Shhh. Let's be very quiet and not disturb the sleeping beauty."

"Hunh?" Grontunk's voice was astounded.

"I just put big brother to sleep. All of his 'natural functions' like breathing—pulsing, feeding us, and essential operations are working fine. But the only reason I was arguing with that particular section was to find out which section it was so I could temporarily cool it for a citizen's own good."

Murtag seemed horrified. "You mean—you *cooled* the computer?"

"Yep. Let's go."

With Terry leading the way they all converged on the in-world transposer control room.

"Which box do we step into?" Grontunk asked.

"Whoa down, boy. We've got about twenty-four hours work here rewiring these things so we can change the kickback function. Then we'll make some tests, sending things through with us far, far away from this room. You recall our little explosion?"

"Quite vividly," said Murtag.

"Well, I suspect that's one of the things that can happen with the regular transposer field—if the terminal at the far end isn't set up to phase out the field. The power that takes you through has got to be absorbed somewhere, you know. If the absorber in the far terminal's not working, it's apt to surge the hell back here and leave a hole in this base bigger than we are. So we'll fix this transposer to work as an 'explorer' circuit, with all the controls and power absorption on this end. It wouldn't really be proper to dust ourselves all over Government Planet and blast out our own base at the same time, just in case the Government's not on its electronic toes."

"Not that I want to find out by experiment, Terry," Grontunk said, "but could a *regular* transposer field explode like yours did?"

"Quite like that," Terry said; "only, since this transposer field would be bigger than the ones we were playing with, and would contain a large amount instead of mere increments of mass, the explosions would likewise be bigger —though I suspect in the larger field we wouldn't really get anywhere near as close to one hundred percent conversion of the mass. Still—the explosion would be quite sufficient to make a dent in the ground, say ten or fifteen stads in diameter." Even as he said it, Terry wondered. Did the galactic word "stad" and the Roman word "stadia" bear some real relation to each other, or were they merely coincidence?

It had taken longer than Terry estimated, and it was three days before they finally stepped through the transposer onto Pranje—into a huge, bowl-shaped depression, much larger than Terry had expected.

The bowl rim, a full twenty stads away, was not quite centered on their landing point, and over toward the center a small lake had gathered in the depression.

Nor, Terry noted, was the rim regular as he had expected. Deep washes and gullies of brilliantly colored sand both gentled the valley with beauty and attested to the passage of time since it had been formed; and everywhere about there were bright shards of glassy material that he recognized as spelling out atomic disaster.

Grontunk broke the silence. "Where's the city?" he asked. "I thought this was Government Center. Why would they have their landing area placed in such a beautiful valley so far away from civilization?"

Terry smiled wryly. "I expect things have changed a bit since this was originally designed," he said.

Again Terry scanned the bowl. There were a few straggling growths, small bushes, but no trees. The air seemed dry, sterile. At least part of the once-lush planet would take more than three hundred and seventy-three Galactic years to recover the verdant forest that had probably grown here before men had intervened, he thought.

"Best we go elsewhere, Terry. It's a bit hot here still. Radioactively, I mean." Tinkan spoke quietly.

"Terry, I've located buildings." Murtag had been using one of the tiny viewpoints. "Over that way," she indicated.

Terry began making some adjustments on his personal transposer, first with the viewpoint, selecting out the roof of the largest building, and then expanding his transposer field to include the group. With the usual lurch they were there.

Around them was an area of wildly growing, twisted and gnarled shrubs, probably a former rooftop garden—like the hanging gardens of Babylon? he wondered; while stretching away in every direction were the overgrown tops of other huge buildings, not all the same height or size, but all built closely together. The growths showed little of the order they must once have had, but the "ground" beneath them had built up over the centuries, and though there were depressions where the roof had caved into rooms below, the sod was deep and spongy and there seemed little danger in walking across it.

They made their way toward a parapet, passing a caved-in stairwell as they went, its steps of stone seeming to stand alone among the debris that choked across it.

The vast expanse spread before them with the appearance of a sea of shrubbery, except for the deep canyons that must once have been streets that they could discern when they looked straight down.

"But we were so young!" Piet's voice beside him sounded small and lonely. "There were so many things to do and learn. So many places to go. So much to explore." She paused for a moment and then went on. "But now? As you've been saying, Terry, a zero. It all came to nothing."

"Not true." Tinkan's remark was almost fierce. "There was a cycle of action here, and the cycle was completed. But the sum of a cycle of action is not zero."

99

"Of course it is." Terry's voice held the horror that he felt. "All equations balance to zero in the end."

"Yes, Friend Terry." Grontunk's Saurian features seemed strangely mature as he, too, gazed over the scene. "But, nevertheless, the sum of a cycle of action—through evolution—is, as Tinkan says, not zero."

"Not . . ." Terry's voice faltered, his mind still held spellbound by the wasted majesty of the past.

"What you see before you," said Tinkan, still fiercely, "was *then* and *theirs*. It is we who are here and now. It is we who will now put the digital factors—the precise details of execution—into the analogue computation that is the universal; that is life."

Terry looked at his companion in growing respect. "You are right," he said. "That"—he waved at the panorama before him—"is not a zero but a heritage. The sum of a cycle of action is the heritage of life; and until and unless evolution ceases and the universe itself returns to zero, no cycle is complete in the mathematical sense. They have left us a heritage, and in their destruction have sown new seeds for the future that other cycles, different cycles, might commence."

"And we," said Tinkan, "are some of those seeds. The next cycle will therefore be by our efforts. Let us hope we can do as well as they."

The spell was broken now, and Terry could survey the past without a feeling or horror and loss, and face the future with hopefulness. "The sum wasn't zero after all. Let's go see what we can do to add to the equation."

He turned from the parapet abruptly, seeking the stairway they'd passed.

Once they'd gotten past the rubble and growth at the entrance, the stairwell itself proved strong enough to hold them, and they entered, Grontunk in the lead. The stairway ended in a narrow passage, and Grontunk stopped before a corner in the passage.

"Pardon me," he said in a small voice, "but it's very dark down there. And . . ."

Murtag giggled, and abruptly there was blazing light from a tiny dot directly over her head. Terry glanced up, then quickly averted his eyes from the brilliance. "Hey, that's a new trick."

"Not really," the girl denied, "just an adaptation of one of your viewpoint ideas." She waved her hand at the ceiling. "A big viewpoint topside, collecting sunlight and sort of squeezing it into this one down here."

"Very effective," Tinkan noted, as another spot of light appeared over his head.

As they turned to proceed down the stairs there was a metallic clank, and Tinkan, in the lead now, stood staring as though in pain, looking at the arm of a robot that he had kicked while passing a pile of debris. Then he was down on hands and knees, scrabbling into the pile of rubble. It was only a few moments before he sat back, the bits and pieces of the robot that he had unearthed a small pile before him.

"I . . ." He hesitated and started again, his voice careful. "I am sorry to have . . . delayed the exploration."

Terry stood staring at the remains of the robot and the bones that had been in the same pile. A child's tiny skull stared back.

XIII

As THEY explored deeper through the old building's service passageways—for citizen passage would have been by the inoperative transposers—the number and preserved condition of the bones and the metalloid robots increased.

At last Tinkan found a robot that he felt might be in condition still to reactivate, and working with what seemed to Terry to be the gentle tenderness of a surgeon, traced the circuits to make sure they were intact, then connected in his spare power supply.

The robot stirred, rose, turned and started to move away. Tinkan spoke to him quietly. "We need information, Entity."

The robot turned to Tinkan, then to Terry. "I seem to have fallen, sir. There may be a malfunction. Shall I send a robot in good repair to you?"

"Thank you, no," said Terry. "I wish you to answer me. How do I reach the . . . Galactic Coordinator?"

101

The robot hesitated. "I don't seem to be in communication with my computer, sir."

"Are your own memory banks functioning?" Tinkan asked.

"Yes, but . . ."

"What was the nature of your mission?"

"Just routine, sir. I was supposed to reset some circuit breakers that have just gone out. I'd better go do that now. There's an extraordinary amount of traffic, and we're all on duty to handle it."

"Can you answer my question?" Terry asked. "The Galctic Coordinator's office. Where is it?"

"Oh no, sir. I've never been there. Why, I've never been out of this building, sir."

"The main power control boards for this building," Terry said. "Can you tell me where those are?"

"Yes, sir. Transposer terminal . . ."

"No, no. The physical location. The transposers aren't working."

"They aren't . . ."

"Take us to the power control room by the service routes."

"Yes, sir. But it's scarcely suitable for a citizen to go that way, sir."

"Do you mean dangerous?"

"Well, no, sir."

"Then let's go."

It turned out not to be very far away, but when they got there it was totally dead.

"I don't understand, sir," The service robot seemed shaken. "It's never gone dead before. Not ever. Perhaps . . . perhaps I'd better go call a Supervisor?"

"And how would you go about that?"

"Why, I . . . I . . ." The robot turned back from a dead communications panel. "I don't know, sir."

It was only a small distribution sub-station that they had entered, with a single check-out board, the type in use back at Base. He seated himself at it and then realized that there would not even be emergency power with which to check.

Working with the tiny viewpoint while the others lighted the room, Terry poked around the panel and eventually got it connected to his own power supply. The panel was in good working order, but the story it gave was of disaster. The supply station to which it had been connected gave no response at all.

"Probably doesn't even exist anymore," Terry said. "The supply stations would have been near the transposer stations."

Working things in the other direction, Terry fed power from his pack through the board and into the building's circuits. Lights came on around them. Terry began testing various functions and hardly noticed when a door behind him opened.

He came to with a start as he felt something touch his shoulder, gently but firmly. A tremendous robot stood there and was saying quietly, "The computer orders that we remove the unauthorized personnel from the control room. Please come with me, sir."

Terry stared up, fear welling through him. Then he shoved the emotion firmly aside and reaching to his belt switched off the power that had activated the panel. The robot stood as he had been when the power was on, his hand still firmly on Terry's shoulder, but unmoving. Terry tried to wrench free, but the grip was unyielding.

"Hey, you!" Terry called to the independently powered servo they had reactivated, "get your buddy here off of me."

"Yes, sir. As soon as I can remove this unauthorized personnel, sir," said the servo, and Terry realized that Grontunk was struggling in the servo's grip.

"Oh, for . . . Tinkan, would you mind explaining to this character who we are and what we're doing here?"

Tinkan lumbered over. "You are interfering with the work of a Supervisor, Servo," he said stiffly. "The computer is and has been out of order except for the few seconds during which it spoke. It was obviously too deranged to recognize the rank of those who were repairing its circuitry."

The servo looked from what appeared to him to be a service robot, to the citizens at hand. "With which computer do you function?" he asked.

"The master, of course," said Tinkan brusquely. "Now

103

please see that the Supervisor and his assistants are un-handed so that they may get on with their tasks."

"Your pardon, sir," said the robot to Grontunk as he released his grip.

Grontunk shook himself, then bowed to the robot. "Quite all right, Hey-you," he said.

Terry smothered a laugh. Well, that took care of naming their new ally, he thought.

Meanwhile Tinkan was standing impassively nearby as though doing nothing. Then Terry felt the massive hand on his shoulder quiver and relax. "Oh, thanks, Tinkan. You did it with your little viewpoint? I should have thought of that one myself."

But Tinkan was still absorbed and did not respond. The robot body near Terry suddenly stepped back, turned and laid itself prone on the floor, and now Tinkan moved to its side.

"This one," he said, "was a computer service robot, and he will know all about the local computer. Just a minute, Terry, while I get those orders about removing unauthorized personnel out of his memory banks. Then I think he may be quite useful to us."

A few minutes later the big robot twitched, moved, flailed his arms, then stood up again. "This way, sir," he said, and with the others following they made their way to the building's computer room.

Terry activated the computer part by part with his power pack, but it took some time before he could piece together the information he needed. Finally it came—the information that the Galactic Coordinator's office was built deep into the planet itself, and could be reached only by transposer. Then the search continued for the coordinates of that office. These were harder to come by, but eventually Terry teased them out. After that it was simply a matter of activating a local transposer with their own power, testing it, then stepping through.

Terry and Tinkan entered alone. The room, lighted and aired by their globes, was austerely sumptuous and only faintly musty. A shrunken, mummified body lay across a huge desk in the corner, mute witness to the fate of the co-

104

ordinator himself. But beneath the mummy's arms was a pile of paper and Terry, almost hesitantly, removed it.

Handwritten, the pages dry and crumbly, a record of what had occurred was theirs at last.

"I leave this record," the notes began, "because, though I have waited now for days, no help has come, no power has been turned back on except the emergency power lights, which are now fading. I am losing hope.

"I am a prisoner—but to what forces I do not know. I cannot get out of this room. If I had been an engineer rather than an administrator, I might be able to find a way out, to save my people from whatever fate has overcome them. But I am an administrator, and the engineers have not restored the power.

"It happened so suddenly. There was no cause of which I know. First there were the beginnings of movement throughout the galaxy. World after world, the movement began, and in the few hours before—the end, I suppose I should call it—we tried to find the cause. We believe a panic started when too many people tried to attend the festival on Treling, and for the first time in Galactic history the transposers there were clogged. Such clogging could not have lasted more than minutes, but that was the first indication we had of what became a vast movement of peoples; a panic movement.

"It swelled and swelled, and I had transcripted orders to go out on all communications channels that citizens were to remain where they were for a short period, regardless of circumstance—anything to stem the flow.

"I had finished transcribing the message, and reached for the communications button and—the power failed. It was many minutes later that my office was shaken by what could have been an earthquake, but what could also have been an explosion.

"Never has either happened before, not since the early days of civilization. We learned long since the necessity to leave stable the magnetic systems of the planets so that areas of magnetic flux did not develop to create earthquakes—and what cause could there have been for an explosion?

"Unless, perhaps, Supervisor Sharley was more right than he knew when he warned me that the interconnectivity of the transposer net was growing too complex—that the interlocking grids might one day react to a single failure in a single grid, and that the resultant surging power would wipe out the network of all the planets in a vast shock wave effect as the power that has sustained us turned against us blindly.

"No. That is impossible, as other supervisors explained to me and I explained to Sharley. But in the event that such an unlikelihood may have been part of whatever has occurred, I hereby outline what he said, and what was denied by every other person in authority that I consulted.

"Sharley told me last month, in an hour-long interview I granted him, that we were cutting the budget too fine; that we were allowing interconnections between transposers without sufficient protection. I agreed in principle that he might be right, and told him I would do something about it—and I did. I consulted others, who denied that this was a hazard; and I found out what modifications would cost. I had not realized when I was talking to him, and I am sure he had not realized, what a really tremendous expenditure it would be to undertake to modify the transposer grid as it has grown up.

"I have, however, made plans that his safeguards will be built into all future transposer stations as we expand. If I understood him correctly, we have not yet reached the limits to which the grids may be interconnected safely, and it seems to me that this provision might be sufficient.

"I mention this only as speculation, since I do not know what has happened; but to whatever Supervisor or technician finds these notes, I pledge you to publish them and to spare no effort to see that we do not again fall into the trap of depending too much on the transposer system of transportation—for whatever else may have occurred, I myself shall be dead because of this error.

"Yet it could not have been the grid system; small breaks would have preceded any major one.

"Then, perhaps, we have been invaded? Perhaps one of the colonial mining worlds has discovered our existence as

106

more—or less—than gods, and has turned on us, using our own 'God-doors' for the invasion? But the barbarians of such planets are incapable either of recognizing us for what we are, or of utilizing such knowledge should they recognize it. No, that too is impossible.

"Then, perhaps, the transposers for bringing in the metals from the mining planets have been built to utilize too great a power surge, to carry too great a load in one movement? And one of them has flashed back—a remote possibility— into an area that has prevented help from reaching me? The trend toward power stations on the mining worlds built with massive marble insulators for their power taps is one I have decried, even though they make possible the lifting of stads of ore in a few transpositions. I assigned Sharley to the task of checking such installations on one planet in the spiral arm, but his report has not reached me yet. Could an explosion from such a heavy transposition have thus isolated me?

"That too, is impossible—yet it is impossible that I am a prisoner. It is impossible that I am dying here for lack of air, though food and water are in abundance. But air—I find myself growing dizzy, for I have probably already used most of the oxygen content. Air was brought by transposition—how else to serve an office in the heart of the planet?

"I should die happier if I could know whether it is just this hole; but the implications of the time that has passed force me to believe that it is the entire area above me— perhaps all of Government Planet—that is without power; and that the planet itself is isolated until someone from another planet finds a way to reach us.

"And if we are isolated, that means that the people of the galaxy are leaderless at this time of panic. I can only hope that the citizens bear themselves well without guidance. . . ."

There was more, but the scribble became illegible, and Terry seemed to see the hands drop from the paper as the Coordinator became dizzier from lack of air. He placed the pages gently back on the desk, feeling as though he had violated a tomb.

107

Turning back to the transposer Terry and Tinkan stepped through into the computer room where they had left the others.

From there, bringing with them the two reactivated robots, they made their way through the desolated building to its roof, across to the huge bowl-like depression, and, activating the radio signal they'd installed on the transposer at Base, back—home. And Terry was filled with a great, wrenching longing for the lush green planet from which he had sprung.

XIV

TERRY WOKE the next morning but did not get up. Instead he lay placing bits and fragments of his dreams together, dreams haunted by scenes of a civilization exploding, by restless, unstilled ghosts that had walked by his side through the night.

Ghosts, he thought, of suicides who had taken their own lives—not from anger, not even for need, but in ignorance.

Terry pictured the population of the great civilization—secure, comforted, dependent; less than one-one-hundredth of one percent had even bothered to school themselves to a mental grasp of the factors of the civilization that was their birthright. If they were not masters of the technology which cradled them, that technology would become, inevitably, their master; a blind master that could only lash out to kill that which had constructed it.

Somewhere along the line somebody had skimped, had decided that one ton of copper could be used where ten might have done a perfect job. Somewhere along the line, a statistician might have allowed for a few million less people than those who had actually gone to attend a spring festival.

Somewhere along the line there had been a single failure, and people, not understanding that failure or the technological reasons for it, had compounded it. Somewhere along the line a thin edge of panic had crept in and cut like a knife at the vitals of a great civilization. Panic had engulfed world after world.

Terry could almost feel the surges of people from planet to planet; the surges of electricity that those people represented; pounding through the individual planetary networks, a shock wave effect; a shock wave as predictable and as violent as a hurricane. A shock wave that could be caused by a very minor potential difference in the random pressures represented by a population of hundreds of billions of individual free-willed entities in a statistical distribution pattern—as a hurricane is caused by a minor potential difference in the random pressures represented by hundreds of billions of molecules in the statistical distribution pattern known as atmosphere.

The power absorption unit on one transposer on one planet had become overloaded and failed, and the power it should have absorbed had lashed back to wipe out the terminal at the far end; and beside that terminal at the far end had been another that, destroyed, had lashed the surge along the grid-ways, the power growing and surging in violent crashes of energy that sought every pathway open to a planet in the galaxy and felled them each, like dominoes, not one after another but on an exponential curve so immediate, with such near-simultaneity, that the entire grid was cremated in what would have appeared to an intergalactic onlooker as one searing flash, though, like lightning, it was made up of a myriad smaller flashes.

It would have been over in seconds, in less than seconds; a civilization that had blanketed the stars consumed in the time between one breathing and the next. And if, by chance, on one single planet no transposer had been in operation at the time, the first attempt to use a transposer would have brought its own unabsorbed energy lashing back to add that planet, too, to the list of deadened worlds.

How could it have happened? Terry asked himself, but even as he asked another part of his mind knew coldly that, granted the facts that had existed, it couldn't have failed to happen. The equations were there, and the mathematics of those equations spelled it out in hard, inescapable terms. The condition had existed; the catastrophe was inevitable.

What, then, had protected this outpost station? A furious child and an implacable computer. The fact that a young

109

girl had become frantic and pulled a switch, probably just moments before the catastrophe occurred; and that, after that, before a transposition had been attempted, the computer had sent a message out, calling a supervisor. The flashback from just the message had destroyed one power unit, and the computer had refused to try again.

Yes, statistically, some would have survived. Statistically, there must be planets out there with people who were smart enough to yet be still alive. Statistically, the patient might yet survive, provided someone came along and offered first aid.

Each of us—the survivors—must win his own way to the highest technology with which he is able to cope—with the highest that he desires; and then, as a responsible adult, live within that, he thought.

But a man must understand, must be master, of the factors which control his life—or else be a slave. And we who have survived will be slaves to neither man nor machine.

XV

IT WAS Murtag who suggested that it would be faster and easier to investigate the other planets by an extension of the viewpoint system instead of personal exploration, and the suggestion had proved valid.

There were planets that were still ravaged and sterile; there were those where great forests and plains had replaced any trace of civilization. There were some where the natives were just beginning the use of fire and tools. Though many of the three hundred planets they had so far investigated were inhabited, less than ten percent proved to have any level of civilization worth a second glance. On some, there were still remnants, easily identifiable traces of the old civilization; on other, rougher worlds, remnants of the old civilization were practically nonexistent.

Murtag's University Planet of Haizen, a tropical world of small islands, their beaches lapped by azure waters, had developed a carefree, relaxed tribal system that reminded Terry of Earth's South Sea Islanders. He "listened in" to

110

one of their religious ceremonies and found them praying to the "Great Supervisor" to return and wash them of their sins, but their religious attitudes didn't seem to bother them other than during ceremonies.

There was a forbidding world of massive stone forts and snowy forests, and a forested world where the people lived in tribal groups of tents.

On the more technologically advanced worlds, which he spent much time exploring and trying to understand, a factor seemed to exist which puzzled him intensely. Many of these seemed to have reached toward their former technological ability and to have fallen back, not once but again and again; while others seemed to have taken small steps toward technology and then frozen, advancing no further, simply to hold where they were.

"There doesn't seem to be any reason," Terry said to Murtag, "why some of these worlds haven't advanced all the way up to their original levels." He waved toward the bright image of a small city where both electricity and radio were used, but where their use had remained static, so far as he could tell, for a very long span of time. "It's almost," he mused, "as though someone were mixing them up."

He glanced up and saw Murtag looking at him with a peculiar intensity, and he smoothed the subject obliquely with the viewpoint still focused on the bustling activity of the small city. "We know that some technology survived. The question now becomes what to do about it?"

"What do you plan to do about it, Terry?" Murtag asked softly.

It was the accent on the you that focused Terry's attention finally on the alarm bells that had rung more than once at the back of his mind over the weeks, as tiny anomalies occurred. The first time was when there'd been her reference to books, quickly changed to tapes. All information had been microfilmed for reader tapes in the old civilization; "books" was a concept she would have had to meet with later. And there'd been the computer's mid-sentence refusal to tell him how long it was permitted to keep a citizen cooled; a refusal that had come too late for him to escape the conclusion that there was a limit to that time,

111

and that the limit would certainly be less than three hundred and seventy-three years.

He phased out the viewpoint and turned to her fiercely. "You are a ringer," he said. "You pulled the switch that saved this outpost, and you were probably cooled for it, but—how long were you cooled? You were released, and you found your way out of the trap, because—you are a ringer."

There was a laugh bubbling at the back of Murtag's voice as she asked, "What trap, Terry? And what makes you think I'm a ringer?"

"Any number of things, but mostly what I have decided should be done about the situation here. If I were a supervisor, I would set up a system. A mouse trap, so to speak, that would attract those people of the highest scientific ability who also had the curiosity to investigate minor anomalies. I wouldn't make my mouse trap inaccessible to more chancy catches"—he bowed toward Grontunk —"such as our Saurian friend here who seems to have fallen into it much more by accident than I did. Nor would I make my mouse trap so obvious that persons in a technical civilization would fall into it wholesale.

"I would place it in such a way that if someone disappeared in its vicinity there could be a ready explanation in the form of 'natural causes' for a such a disappearance, say next to the raging torrent of a mountain stream, where an investigator might be presumed to have slipped on the rocks, fallen and been swept away. I have not checked with Grontunk as to the physical aspects of the spot from which he departed his world, but I expect it was similarly situated. Am I right?"

"A very apt description," Grontunk answered promptly. "Such a place as the one I disappeared from was inaccessible to begin with and considered highly dangerous territory so that someone lost within it would not likely be found."

"And what would you do with the people you mouse trapped?" Murtag asked with a broad smile.

"Not a thing. I would put them in a position where they could learn if they had the initiative and drive to overcome obstacles that would be imposed on their freedom

112

to learn. And if they showed signs of learning, I would send a tutor"—he nodded toward Murtag—"to monitor the process of learning, but not to interfere with it."

"And if they didn't learn?"

"I would leave them well cared for in a completely automatic environment and wait."

"Terry, you mean that's what they were going to do with me?" Grontunk asked.

"I suspect so. You'd been here for five Galactic months and you hadn't made much headway with understanding the computer. Maybe eventually you would have raised enough hell so that they would send somebody like Murtag around to find out about it. But in the event you didn't —well, it wouldn't have been a good idea to send you home. That might give away the mouse trap."

"We have a planet where Grontunk would have been happy. He'd have been sent there in another month." Murtag's voice was gay. "But tell me, Terry, having set up this 'mouse trap,' as you call it, what would have been your purpose?"

"Not quite yet. Let me add in a few more of the technical details first. Having mouse trapped somebody that showed enough ability to attempt to solve the problem by force or any other means, I would then, as I said, send in a tutor. The tutor would exercise a very minimum of control, preferably none at all, until the mouse trapped student got to the point where he was actually capable of doing something. When the student was capable of actively interfering in that mess out there"—Terry waved toward the darkened viewscreen—"the tutor would then have to be very careful indeed. It would be safe enough to direct the student to one of the dead worlds like Pranje. It would then, however, be the tutor's job to point out that further investigations were dangerous and how to conduct them safely—safely, not from the viewpoint of the student's safety, but from the viewpoint of not upsetting things out there too much.

"You have, in effect, here"—Terry gestured to indicate the computer complex—"such a mouse trap. I assume that it is set up as a sieve, and designed very carefully to pass

113

only those people that you're looking for. I assume, since you haven't cooled me yet, that I am one of those people. I will even go so far as to assume that Earth may have been a former mining planet for your great galactic civilization."

Murtag started to interrupt but Terry went on. "That assumption is not, however, necessary to my case, since I would extend such a mouse trap not only to the old planets but to any new planets I located which showed signs of growing intelligence.

"I also assume that there is a definite purpose behind this sieve. I assume that someone set it up because they had forecast a disaster and had prepared for it. I assume that they have determined the basic equation that freedom must inevitably be in proportion to responsibility." Murtag was shaking her head but Terry went on, "And the corollary of that statement: that you cannot have, or maintain, a free society full of irresponsible people.

"I assume that the shock wave was quite real and not caused, at least not caused in the sense of someone pulling a switch. The equations were there; it would not have been necessary to cause the disaster, nor could it have been prevented.

"The purpose of the mouse trap, or sieve, or whatever you wish to call it, is simplicity itself—to select the most able individuals as supervisors to maintain the knowledge of civilization until the civilization shall grow up to reinherit that which it lost by default."

Again Murtag was shaking her head, but Terry said, "You're doing exactly what the computer said: making a set of Supervisors."

"Terry"—the smile was gone from Murtag's voice now—"I've never heard a better outline of the reasons we should be following. But you're wrong in one aspect of your analysis. We have not set ourselves up as custodians, and several of the points that you just made are completely foreign to our thinking Your talk of freedom and responsibility in terms of the people out there"—she too, gestured at the viewscreen—"is just as foreign to our concepts as the idea of independently powered and free robots was to me when you first introduced me to the concept.

"We are making Supervisors, as you say, by a mouse trap system. We also take samples of beings from cultures occasionally just for study and scientific purposes.

"And—yes, I was mouse trapped, although right at the beginning and quite by accident; and I worked my way through the trap.

"But—quite contrary to your concept that we keep you or ourselves from interfering in the developing cultures out there—we consider it our job to interfere in and change each culture that we supervise; to force their growth until they throw off geniuses for us to pick, before they die back down of the forced growth.

"We're using the planets as genetic pools to breed our kind—a superior race *capable* of civilization.

"You have, by the way, introduced several new concepts into our program. The use of the transposer field, as we're using it here, is an old method, but we did not have the formulas for the tiny screens, or the tiny viewpoints, or the control over them that you have developed.

"Nor had they thought seriously of free entities like Tinkan. They thought they knew the robot's capabilities and limitations"—suddenly it was *they*, not *we* of whom she spoke, Terry noted—"and those capabilities and limitations they have decided are similar in many respects to those that will be allowed the people.

"They have decided," she went on in a flat voice, "that the people's only function is to provide the occasional highly intelligent individual for them to strain off. They have interfered time and time again in the hope of creating stresses and pressures, interminglings, cross-diversions—forcing the races to produce exceptional products by threats to their survival, then removing the exceptional products so that each race reverts time and again to savagery."

As Terry watched the girl's face the image of a little man danced between them—a little man with a paint-brush moustache screaming to a hypnotized audience the doctrine of the "Master Race," while millions went to the gas chambers.

The ghostly echo from the hypnotized populace came back to him: "Sieg Heil!"

"Your idea for free entities from among the robots—it upset them. They had not considered the robots capable of evolving, and they have decided it must not be permitted. Some of them were so horrified that I have had to delete much from my reports in order to keep them from 'stopping' you. I have convinced them that they can stop the result of the experiment later. . . ."

Terry rose unsteadily from the table, his face wooden. "Thank you, Murtag," he said formally.

"*Terry*. . . ." It broke from her like a cry, but he turned away.

"I'm going to my quarters for—for computation," he said.

Terry lay on the bed forcing his mind away from the scene he'd just left; needing to wash his mind clean of the concepts he'd been listening to.

Home, he thought, and willed a picture of cool, green Earth into his mind.

In all these Galactic months he'd not found out where it was. Well, that was easy. The computer knew.

Without so much as twitching a muscle Terry sent a viewpoint probe into the computer's memory compartment. It was a matter of minutes to locate the coordinates. But which station? And then he realized it didn't matter. The coordinates for the planet itself were enough for him.

But wait, there was evidence of tampering here. New Earth stations had been set up as recently as a Galactic year ago. Quickly Terry sent the tape scuttling back to other references to Earth coordinates. There it was, the original, and that checked in time. It was dated before the collapse. But the new ones, the ones he had puzzled over, were comparatively recent.

Well, he could search it more closely later.

Reaching out with the tiny viewpoint, Terry was away from base and out among the stars, and the coordinates—well, he seemed to have gotten pretty close. There was a bright yellow G-O type sun. Carefully he adjusted coordinates.

The sun was closer and blue-green, painfully, wonderfully familiar Earth hung below him.

Now with the close reference point, it was easy. Swiftly Terry dropped the viewpoint in toward the coastline of California, and Berkeley seemed to spread out as though he were coming up on it with a zoom lens. With an odd sensation of semi-familiarity, Terry admired the scene. The city of Berkeley with the great Bay Bridge spiderwebbing out toward Frisco.

Why not give Cal a surprise, he thought. He should be getting out of classes about now.

With a rapidity that startled even Terry when it occurred in familiar territory, the scene shifted, the tiny dot moving through the air as though it weren't there. A ground observer, he thought wryly, if he could have seen a dot so small, would have thought it moved at better than 2,000 miles an hour; much as the focus end of a searchlight beam can be observed to flee across the horizon far faster than a jet plane could fly.

Dropping lower, Terry allowed the viewpoint to come up to the window of a classroom where Cal might be. It was deserted—so deserted that it had an unused look about it that startled Terry. Then he laughed. Summer, he thought. And Cal lived—where? He wasn't sure.

He thought of looking it up in a phone book, but the limitations of the little viewpoint would make that a very difficult feat indeed. He might be able to flip the book open, but getting the address would be a long and tedious task.

So, he thought, go to a phone and call an operator? But why not simply go to an operator?

Terry was having fun.

Withdrawing the viewpoint to a height, he scanned around until he located the telephone exchange, then zoomed on to it. Carefully he phased the dot through the roof and found himself in an enclosed crawlway. Dropping lower, he found himself among rack after rack of automatic dial equipment. Dropping again, he found at last the large switchboard room with operators monitoring the busy system.

That's a cute one over there, Terry decided, and moved the tiny viewpoint closer, then up next to the headset. Then

117

he phased it carefully through and into the headphone.
The headphone was busy, and Terry waited paitently until the operator had finished telling a woman that, no ma'am, she had no record of a Joe's Market at that address, and yes, ma'am, she'd looked it up under every spelling she could think of.

As the operator cleared the line, Terry spoke up.

"Operator, I'd like the number of Calvin Thorpe. I don't know the address, but it's in Berkeley."

Automatically the operator began looking up the number, and Terry backed the viewpoint out of the headset in. order to see the address.

"Your number is . . ." Then she noticed that she was not connected into a circuit. "I beg your pardon, sir. To whom am I talking?"

Terry moved the tiny dot down past her nose to get a closer look at the page in front of her, and at the same time muttered, "Don't worry about it. I'm just an intergalactic spy."

The operator shrieked and swatted, and Terry managed to duck just in time—at least it felt like ducking as he moved the viewpoint from the range of the downcoming hand.

Then, having picked up the address and observing a matronly woman approaching, he moved up again behind the girl's ear. "Don't admit a thing," he muttered. "Tell her it was a bee."

"Yes, sir," she said in a small voice, and as the chief operator came close, "I'm sorry, Mabel, it was a bee."

"Nonsense, my dear, we never permit bees in our switchboard."

Terry backed the viewpoint off, moved it behind the matronly figure, and proceeded to demonstrate that sometimes bees could get into switchboard works. Then he hastily withdrew, leaving an uproar of screams and confusion behind.

Cal's apartment was not far away—as the viewpoint flies, thought Terry—and it was only a few minutes later that he was hanging outside a window observing.

There didn't appear to be anybody home, but that was

118

some nice equipment Cal had. Carefully, Terry phased the viewpoint through the window and moved over to examine the ham rig more closely. . . .

Ham rig? Suddenly he had a sense of *déjà vu*—of having been here before. A ham rig it was, on the surface. But underneath—Terry closely examined some of the dials that didn't seem to be what they said they were, and then phased the viewpoint behind the panel.

They *weren't* what they said they were. Some of the rigging definitely was ordinary ham outfit circuitry; but the rest . . . Terry found himself gazing at components that he knew—not from the past, but from the present! These were components made by the old civilization; components that had no reason to be on Earth, or at least none that Terry knew. The transposer circuit he was examining was a different modification, but nevertheless a modification, of the ones with which he was familiar. Not so compact as Terry's own device, but not so large and cumbersome as the originals.

On the desk a telephone began to ring, and as Terry moved the viewpoint back through the panel he saw a tiny needle flickering with each ring. A signal? Abruptly Cal materialized beside the desk and walked to his chair to answer the telephone.

So that's how it works, Terry thought. *But why?*

The phone conversation was brief, and Cal turned toward the "ham rig"—then froze, staring directly at Terry—at the viewpoint, Terry realized, although it felt as though Cal's eyes were staring directly into his own.

Cal's face blanched, but he spoke calmly.

"So you've found me," he said. "And I know there's no point in running." He stepped back from the dot as though revolted by its presence.

"Your techniques are getting better," he continued, as though talking to hear himself talk, "I didn't know you rats had such good control over the transposer field." He was edging toward the side of the desk, now.

"Who's a rat?" Terry asked.

"Who's a . . . *who are you?*"

The whiteness began to leave Cal's face and a note of hope entered his voice. "Quick, quick—who are you?"

"You know me, Cal. Terry. Terry Ferman."

"My God—thank God!" Then, with a quick control that fell on him like a blanket, "Terry, lad! I'd given you up for lost. It's been . . . it's been . . ."

"It's been a long time," Terry said flatly. "But I want to know—right now, quick—who you thought I was. *And keep your hand off that panel.*"

"Such a small viewpoint. The smallest we've been able to manage is still nearly fifteen feet in diameter." Cal had relaxed a bit and moved away, as Terry had suggested, from the side panel of the desk, but he was still staring at the black dot with an intensity that belied any lightness his voice might hold. "They . . . they have nothing like this either," he continued. "You must have been very busy, lad." Then with what was barely disguised as casualness in his voice, "You *are* still independent, aren't you? But no." The note of hope, if it had been hope, fell out of the voice. "I forget. It was *their* trap you fell into."

"*Terry! Look out!*" Murtag's voice, a near scream, came from almost beside his ear—not his viewpoint ear, but the ear on his head on the bed at Base. Terry had almost forgotten that he wasn't at Berkeley with Cal, but his automatic responses were quicker than his returning senses, and even as he reoriented himself he was phasing his viewpoint out of existence, was relaxing on his bed at "home base."

And there was a stranger standing in the doorway, stunner in hand, finger whitening on the trigger.

With a single gesture, Terry materialized the viewpoint and hurtled it across the room, straight into the muzzle of the stungun. With a crashing roar the gun exploded.

The stranger cursed and began backing away, and Terry danced the viewpoint across in front of his eyes. "Just hold it right there," he said. "Right there. Don't move." Then, as the stranger complied, "Now suppose you tell me what this is all about."

"I thought you . . ." The figure vanished.

"Damn!" Terry swore. "Cops and robbers can get real complicated with these gadgets."

"Oh, that's okay, Terry," Grontunk's voice came from the hall. "I put him in a cooler chamber for you. He was obviously irrational."

Terry felt a bubble somewhere in his throat and did his best to hold it back, but burst out laughing. "Thank you, Grontunk. Murtag?"

A tiny black dot, perched on the wall beside Terry's head, answered. "Yes?"

"Shall we run first or ask questions?"

"Let's run, Terry. I think my former bosses are a bit annoyed with you right now."

"Where's Tinkan?"

"Right here, Terry." A black dot called attention to itself by moving up and down before Terry's eyes.

"A guy's got no privacy at all these days. Dangerous thing, though, privacy."

"We all came in when Murtag said you were in trouble."

"Okay. Everybody over to the old power station. Bring your own atmosphere. It's pretty well wrecked."

As the old power station materialized around him, Terry counted noses. Murtag, Grontunk, Tinkan and Hey-you. "Where's Big Fellow?" Terry asked.

"He said somebody'd got to stay here to take care of the computer, and he's pretty sure 'they' don't know he's not connected."

"Right. Murtag, who was that fellow? You said something about a former boss?"

"There's not much time, Terry. But yes, a former boss. We've been—as they would put it—giving you your rope to see what you would develop. But they decided you were getting too familiar with the computer's tapes—you *were* in there checking coordinates tonight, weren't you?"

"I see. And has this mysterious group got all the data on everything I've been developing?" Terry was suddenly furious.

"No, Terry. They haven't." Murtag smiled. "I haven't been reporting most of it. But they'll get it from the computer tapes."

"The hell they will!" Terry concentrated for a moment and on the other side of the planet a small glow appeared

121

in the computer's tape room; a small glow that spread and danced and there were tapes that were left and tapes that were not.

"How long before they send somebody else?"

"I don't know, Terry."

"Then best we get out of here."

Carefully Terry remembered the coordinates, and the viewpoint jumped. There was the yellow G-O sun. Carefully he shifted. The planet, the blue-green planet. Then closer—the broad stretch of the Pacific—an island.

"Okay. Let's go."

Terry's local field expanded to include the group; and then there was sand and water and a large grove of palms.

XVI

"THEY'LL TRACE us, Terry." Murtag looked wistfully out over the wide blue of the Pacific ocean. "Your home world?" she asked. "Aeryth, you call it?"

"It's a big world," Terry said. "They may have fun tracing us here."

"And yet it may be easier than you think," she countered. "They know the coordinates from which you originally arrived." She shuddered. "And they have their ways."

"Who is this mysterious 'they'?" Terry leaned back against a palm and then as an afterthought, said, "Just a minute."

Concentrating on the tiny viewpoint, Terry swept it up and away from the island. He scanned the waters, and then moved east, slightly north—and there was the coast of California. Down, and there was the Bay Bridge. . . .

Cal was still standing beside the desk where Terry had left him, sorting papers and stuffing them into a briefcase. It hadn't been, he realized, more than ten minutes since their conversation had been cut short.

Without speaking, Terry took careful aim and engulfed the figure—then Cal was on the beach a short distance before him, still with his back turned, frozen in the act of picking up a paper, and staring at the water.

122

Then in one motion Cal twisted, his hand reaching for his belt, and Terry was glad he hadn't dropped him closer. "Relax," he said. "We're independents."

Slowly, Cal came out of the Karate crouch. "Well. Terry lad. Another new trick? You have been learning fast. And I see you've brought some assistants with you." Cal frowned. "I hope you're not planning on introducing the Saurian to any of our local populace? Nor the robots either. Whichever side you're on, we don't play that way."

"That's what I'm trying to find out, Cal. And I invite you to sit a while and spell it out. What rules do you play by?"

"Why don't you ask your Piet there?" The girl flushed furiously. "She should know some of the rules."

Terry's voice took on a hard note. "That's right. And I just did. But then it occurred to me you might not both be on the same side. And I'd like to find out how many hands are being played in this game. You," he went on, speaking to Cal, "*put* me in danger without warning. *She* has saved my life. Yet I gather her pals play rough and foul. And yours? Spell it out, Cal. I'm still independent and i hold a few cards. And I'd like to know what the stakes are."

Cal dropped into a cross-legged sitting position under the palm by which he had been standing. "Okay, I expect I owe you an explanation. You used to think I was kidding when I said there were mysterious forces playing games here on Earth. And I was bound by oath, so I couldn't really tell you. I didn't mean to send you into danger, and for that I apologize, though your mission was real enough —to locate as exactly as we could their trap point. One by one, all over the world, we have been locating those points and backlashing them. But it's a pretty hopeless job.

"I see you know about the transposer field, so I'm telling you nothing new when I mention backlash. And I'm probably telling you nothing new if I mention that there's more than a thousand—many more than a thousand—old stations from which they can set up trap points on planets like Earth.

"You were helping me," he continued, looking down at

the sand, "and you would have been rewarded for it. But I never meant to put you in danger, and I never meant that you should find out so much.

"My group"— he looked at Murtag—"has been fighting hers for a long time; blowing out their traps, trying to stop their interference."

"For what reason," Terry asked softly, "are you trying to stop their interference? It was my understanding that they're attempting to bring about an evolutionary upcurve."

"Exactly," Cal cut in. "They are trying to force evolution. And that we cannot afford. I assume you've seen what happened to the old civilization? We cannot afford ever again to permit such a complex civilization to develop. We must hold back the planets, the people, Terry, for their own good. Only a very few of us should ever be permitted to know the ancient secrets. This world"—he waved his hand vaguely toward the ocean—"already knows too much. They're trying to get too big. We've got to hold them in check, Terry. Keep life simple. For their sake, as well as ours."

"And how do you do this?" Terry asked.

"Any—way—we—can."

"Spell it out, Cal. Spell it out in terms of Earth."

"You can see for yourself, if you want to look, what we've been doing." Then, "The wars are theirs, though. That's their way—what they call forcing evolution. We just work to hold back technologies that are too far in advance—keep them from developing."

"Spell it out in terms of individuals."

Cal shuddered. "Wherever possible, we give them a chance, of course. But they can be discouraged—secrecy— make too great an advance impossible by muzzling the technologists, by isolating them, one from another." He shrugged. "The fate of the race is of more concern than the fate of the individual, Terry."

"Wars and rumors of wars," Terry muttered, "and invisible chains of ignorance with which to hold slaves. It's not a pretty picture, Cal. Not from either side."

Then he turned to Murtag. "I thought Cal was my friend, and I love you beyond any concept of love I ever had. But—damn you both!

124

"I am a free entity, and from no man will I take his freedom—from no being will I take his freedom. I will stand with those who assume for themselves the responsibilities of freedom, and I will let no being take it away from me—or from them.

"So I guess I go my way alone; or with any *free* beings that wish to go with me." His glance swept the robots and the Saurian.

There was a snarl from Cal. "You would set—those—free? You cannot," he said; "they are tied to computers. Or have you miniaturized computers as well? How you are keeping robots running so far from a computer complex I cannot imagine. But also I cannot permit it."

Suddenly there was a needle-pointed weapon in Cal's hand. "I told you we cannot play the game—*that way.*" Darting a brief glance at the sky, he continued, "My friends have located me now. And I will ask you to come quietly. I do not want to hurt you, but I warn you against trying to get away."

Terry's eyes raised and focused on the immobile, saucer-shaped field hanging above them. He was only vaguely aware of the disappearance of something before him as he set his own viewpoint hurtling into and through that field. Briefly he was aware of a roomful of people—no, not full, not really full. There were five old men and a couple of young technicians.

Without hesitation Terry darted his viewpoint at the control panel before which they sat, touched buttons even as the young technician was trying to respond, then without bothering to phase he punched a hole through the panel and into the circuitry beyond, ripping through and destroying the controls.

Then his viewpoint was back in the room. "You gentlemen have a reputation for playing rough," he said. "Let this be a warning. I could have lashed you through your viewpoint. But I did not. This time. I shall even return your agent, if he desires to come back. But I warn you. Interference with me or mine may, next time, be a fatal error on your part."

125

Only then did Terry bring his viewpoint—and his attention—back to the island.

"Where's Cal?" he asked.

"He was acting irrational." There was a gurgle in Grontunk's snort. "So I cooled him for our free beingness's own good."

"Well, get him back here."

It was only an instant before Cal stood before them again, spluttering and looking slightly drowned.

"Er . . ." said Grontunk. "I didn't really have a handy place to stasis him so I—well, I figured he could swim."

Terry turned to the wet figure. "You know our position. How do you choose now?"

Cal looked up to the empty sky; looked back to the five before him, and hesitated only briefly. With a gesture he put on his relaxed manner. "I'll go with you, of course, lad," he said. "If . . ." But he had disappeared.

Terry turned toward Grontunk, about to scold him for this interference, when Tinkan spoke up.

"There was no thought of choice from your Cal. I have sent him back to his masters."

Terry nodded. "And your choice . . . ?"

"You know how I choose, Terry. From the time you first introduced me to the idea."

"Hey-you?"

"Same choice, Terry."

"Grontunk?"

"I never did learn about slavery. And I don't think I want to."

"Murtag?"

Small, determined, her voice trembling with emotion, Murtag answered. "Where you go, I shall go. What you do, I shall do. You cannot go alone, for I shall be with you . . . ."

Terry, furious, about to say something, checked and stumbled. The enormous formality of what she was saying was borne home to him, the old ritual, pagan formality by which a woman was bound.

". . . I shall lay my life before you that your path will be easy, my life and all my possessions. I shall . . ."

126

So that, too, had been one of their tricks; binding their women to their unquestioned will, a slavery more abject . . .

His fury broke into violence and he seized her arms, shaking her to stop the sentences. "No!" he cried, his bitterness choking his words. "No! Not ever! I accept no slaves!"

Her voice had stopped and the tears were coursing down her cheeks as she looked up at him.

"Of your own free choice only," he said. "Of your own free choice at every turn. As an equal and a partner. How, then, do you choose?"

And she was in his arms.

www.ingramcontent.com/pod-product-compliance
Lightning Source LLC
Chambersburg PA
CBHW022034170626
46808CB00003B/1202